TOO CLOSE TO THE LION

TOO CLOSE TO THE LION

A tale of ruthless ambition, love and treachery

JAY PERUMAL

authorHOUSE®

AuthorHouse™ UK Ltd.
1663 Liberty Drive
Bloomington, IN 47403 USA
www.authorhouse.co.uk
Phone: 0800.197.4150

Published by AuthorHouse   01/03/2014

ISBN: 978-1-4918-8698-4 (sc)
ISBN: 978-1-4918-8697-7 (hc)
ISBN: 978-1-4918-8699-1 (e)

*Dedicated to the brave men and women
who dared to venture across oceans from
the land of their birth*

Cherish your own worth
Rather than what you possess!
Contain your own sanity
Rather than the world's riches!
Safeguard your own purity
Rather than your attachments—
And realize my dears that
In the midst of this divine play,
Within the folds of your every role
You will come face to face
One day—at one blessed moment
With the love of loving God!

TOO CLOSE TO THE LION

The year was 1860. India was in the hands of Great Britain. The new conquerors were well on their way to upsetting the Indian economic apple cart. Even the once unassailable kings and princes, bowed to the pressures of the conquerors. Their wealth and their armies were forcibly reduced. Indian art was no longer patronized and the domestic handicrafts industry no longer brought in revenue. India's woes were aggravated by the industrial revolution in England; England was transformed into a super power. The steam engine, the railway, mechanization and other inventions did little to ease the plight of the Indian peasants. India's indigenous industries came under threat from the extensive import of British manufactured goods. Craftsmen found themselves displaced and joined the swelling ranks of the unemployed. But the country was interesting. The lush greenery of rolling hills and valleys, and its expansive green fields, interspaced with quadrangular demarcated boundaries of wet paddy rice fields reflected the bounteous nature of Mother India. Dark skinned, turbaned men, limping along dusty roads, bent double under the yoke of pails of water, were a common sight.

Chandra Chosaran was a young man, nudging thirty years of age. His tall lanky frame and arms rippling with lean muscle from constant toiling on the fields gave him an athletic look, conspicuously different from most of the Indians who were emaciated and gaunt. He was quite unlike his fellow countrymen who almost always wore a turban. His hair, though unkempt, was thick and black with slight soft curls which complemented his thick bushy moustache and matching beetling eyebrows. The white *dhoti,* the only item of traditional garb was somehow quite incongruous on him. He was happy with himself, at least for the moment. The rains were good and the fields had yielded a healthy crop. There was enough to feed his entire extended family and even a surplus to be sold at the local market. But he knew that these were brief moments of relief. He was acutely aware of fact that life was becoming increasingly difficult—survival was becoming a battle.

He would not be able to sustain his family on what mother Earth alone could provide and they faced the very real threat of being displaced as farmers. Because of the system of Indian land tenure—*zamindari* and *ryotwari*, small peasant farmers like them, faced increasing debts. This system demanded that a percentage of the gross produce of the agricultural land be paid as tax to the British colonial Government. While the stipulated percentage was fixed at one-third of the gross produce, the levy was not based on actual revenues from the produce of the land, but instead on an estimate of the potential of the soil. The reality, therefore, was that in some cases more than half of the actual production was appropriated. In the late 18th century the British colonialists instituted the payment of the land tax in cash, rather than in kind. Cultivators were now forced to seek employment in order to pay the land tax or face the very real threat of losing their land, especially when crops failed. The fact that the British agricultural policy encouraged the growth of commercial crops, such as tea, rather than food crops, compounded the problem further. Practising subsistence farming was becoming increasingly difficult. Many resorted to borrowing money from moneylenders who often exploited the plight of the farmers.

Chandra knew that he had to find employment. But in the present economic climate, this too, was difficult. He walked pensively along the dusty road, rutted by parallel tracks of ox-drawn carts. The family cottage constructed of mud and boulders lay tucked away a mile down the road amidst old, twisted and gnarled mango and syringa trees. Chandra was still deep in thought when he stole past his younger brother, Kandan, who sat on a sheepskin rug on the floor, with his chin propped on his fist. His mother, a portly woman with very rotund features, which emphasized her gentleness, was stoking the fires with the bellows to prepare the evening meal. Shubnum, whom he had taken as his wife was seated on the floor, with her legs folded gracefully beneath her loose fitting sari. The end of her sari was draped over her head as she continued patting and rolling the *roti*.

His father, Venketappu, a lanky, gaunt man who sported a bushy, white moustache, which contrasted starkly against his chocolate brown face, sat on the floor, with folded legs in the lotus position, characteristic of someone who was meditating.

"*Chandra!*" he called with an air of authority.

There was an unusual sense of urgency in the old man's voice. Chandra turned around in respectful response. The old man tapped the floor next to him, inviting Chandra to be seated.

"*Kanganis* *were here!*" he said in Hindi.

It was common knowledge that the *kanganis* were recruiting labourers to work in cane fields in lands far off-leagues across the oceans.

Chandra assumed his seat respectfully next to his father.

"*It is becoming increasingly difficult to survive!*"

His father continued to stare fixedly ahead of him as he spoke.

"*Our English masters are here to serve themselves. We are no more than conquered masses to be exploited.*"

The old man sniffed and blew his nose volubly using the end of his *caftan*. "*England grows at the expense of our beloved India. India becomes impoverished through each passing day.*"

The mood was solemn. Chandra too, made no eye contact with his father and waited for a reasonable pause before he spoke.

"What are we to do, father?"

The old man turned to look pointedly at his son and pronounced,

"Natal! There's food and money aplenty!"

Chandra felt the cold fingers of dread claw at the base of his belly. Kandan, too, snapped out of his contemplative reverie, to focus attention on them. It was common knowledge that the British Colonial Government was seeking labour to work in the cane fields of South Africa where Natal was a colony. Stories of the rich prospects in this foreign land, more than ten thousand miles away across the oceans, abounded in every town and village in India. But this had not detracted Chandra from the intensity of his emotions fuelled by his patriotism to India and his kinship to his family.

He gritted his teeth and pursed his lips to control the smouldering anger within him.

"Father!" he hissed between clenched teeth. *"The English are foreigners to this land—a land that we have occupied since time immemorial. They have come from a land that's thousands of miles over the seas. We are in larger numbers—they are few, and yet we have allowed ourselves to be subjugated and oppressed by these people. They have no business in our land, father!"*

The old man listened intently. There were no visible signs of any emotion save for the slight bristling of his moustache.

"My son!" the old man spoke softly and deliberately. *"You have the blood of a warrior and the wisdom of a fool! And that is dangerous and shortsighted!"*

"Father!" protested Chandra, but the old man continued, unwaveringly.

"We are on the brink of famine! What chance will the starving masses have against the might of well-fed English, with their superior fire power, despite our numbers?"

His mother stopped stoking the fire, Shubnum stopped rolling the *roti* and Kandan gazed with anxious interest.

"The English are shrewd my son. They have divided our people – brother against brother. Their strength is not absolute. We have become weaker because we are a nation of fragmented people.

We are in the midst of famine. The English are exporting all surplus food to England. Our raw materials are being used in England to generate products that are imported into India. Our local industries are suffering. You cannot find employment here. Soon! Very soon! We will be starving!"

Chandra knew better than to argue. He looked at the old man and his words were hardly audible.

"Father, I have always respected your wisdom and yet I have a strange sense of foreboding."

"What choice do we have my son?"

A teardrop glistened in the dim light of the oil lamp and snaked its way down the old man's face to be lost in the white strands of his moustache. He bowed his head almost in silent resignation and Chandra knew that there was no fight left in the old man.

Chandra placed his hand fondly on his father's shoulder and whispered, *"I will go father but I shall go alone!"*

"No! I am your wife! I shall go where you go!" Shubnum, who had been listening silently all the while, reacted impulsively, at the risk of offending the men, who traditionally saw no place for women in serious discussions of this nature.

"It's a strange land beti with even stranger people!" the mother looked at Shubnum and exclaimed imploringly. The comment by the old lady emboldened Shubnum and opened the way to push harder.

"I know mother but I have to be with my husband!" But how was she to know that destiny had other plans for her?

That night they slept fitfully but not before Shubnum had convinced her husband that she should accompany him to Natal.

There was much activity and discussion over the weeks in preparation for the day and finally it arrived. It was the 5th of July 1860 and the country was still very much in the clutches of the oppressive Indian summer. Chandra awoke to the sound of the crowing of the cock. The rim of the sun was just visible above the green carpet of young cane covering the hills in the east. He felt momentarily buoyant until the thought of separating from his family plunged him into a state of despondency. Shubnum lay curled in the foetal position on the straw bed on the floor. He shook her gently.

"We need to prepare to leave! We have a long journey to the magistrate's office in Calcutta."

"Why the magistrate's office?" enquired Shubnum, between wide yawns.

"The magistrate will have to register us as being suitable for emigration and also to establish whether we are willing to go," explained Chandra.

Within two hours they had packed their meagre belongings into a sack. Kandan was charged with the task of transporting them by ox-cart for at least fifty miles, from Pondicherry to Madras, a distance estimated to be the capacity of the oxen. Thereafter they were expected to complete the remainder of the journey by train to Calcutta. It was at Calcutta that they were scheduled to report to the magistrate's office; the magistrate would be assessing their suitability for emigration. During the waiting period before embarking they would be housed in a depot.

The ox-drawn cart was loaded with hay and water in preparation for the long and arduous trip. Shubnum's parents and younger sister, who lived an hour away on foot, were also there to bid them farewell. The families were burdened with heavy hearts that morning. While Chandra hugged his mother, she cried bitterly. The old man stood aside with a lump in his throat and his eyes were misty. Shubnum's face was wet with tears as she nuzzled up to her mother who stroked her hair lovingly while whispering words of comfort. She broke away from her mother and approached her father and bowed to touch his feet in the traditional manner. Her father, who could have been no more than in his mid-forties, sported a fringe of silvery grey and black hair much like a monk's tonsure. He attempted to speak, instead he embraced her silently.

While Shubnum took leave of her mother-in-law, Chandra sought the blessings of Shubnum's parents both of whom begged him to take good care of Shubnum and to return to them after having made their fortune.

Chandra then approached his father to bid him farewell.

The old man hugged him and thrust a pouch into his hand.

"This isn't much but it is sufficient to help you on your long journey."

The old man's voice was almost a whisper.

"You are going to a land where the Feringhees will be ruling. Do your duty and keep your distance. Do not go too close to the lion, my son! You will not survive the bite. Make your fortune and do not forget your family and return to us! The English will not be here forever! The good lord will take care of things!"

Little did they realize that, that *was* the final farewell.

The oxen pulled laboriously and slowly. The bells around their necks tinkled incessantly and rhythmically with the undulating movement of their bodies. The hypnotic effects of the bells had both Chandra and Shubnum asleep before long.

They were awoken by voices. A man on horseback, attired in clothes characteristic of the Indian upper class, was trotting alongside the cart and engaging Kandan in a tone that was less than pleasant. Kandan was trying his utmost to be rid of him by answering in short monosyllables and sometimes even ignoring him.

"Enjoy what you eat while you are in Bharat. In Natal the white people will feed you beef and pork!" and the man sniggered. Shubnum looked at her husband with concern and tugged the end of her sari closer to her face.

Chandra snatched the whip from Kandan's hand and raised himself to his full height.

"If you know what's good for you, you will ride away now!" Chandra stood brandishing the whip.

"Oh so the indentured coolie has a backbone", he retorted cynically as he prodded the horse with the heel of his sandalled foot. The horse broke into a canter and pulled away. Save for this singular incident, the journey was uneventful, long and tedious. But this short encounter had filled their already uneasy hearts with foreboding and uncertainty for the rest of the journey.

They travelled for many hours, stopping occasionally to relieve themselves or to allow the oxen to drink from the canister of water they carried. Once, they heard the refreshing babble and gurgle of a stream; they deviated from the rutted path and hacked their way through dense foliage, towards the sound which led to a stream with a healthy flow of refreshingly cool, clear water. They replenished their water canisters and unyoked the oxen to allow them to drink their fill. Having rested sufficiently, they resumed their journey refreshed.

After having travelled for more than six hours, they were exhausted. It was already dark and the sun had set more than two hours earlier. An oil lantern, tied to an upright pole attached to the cart, cast a dim circle of light which shook and shivered with every step of the oxen. When they noticed the comforting glow of a lamp through the open shutters of what appeared to be a farm cottage, Kandan headed for it with renewed strength. The kindly farmer had agreed to put them up for the night, in what appeared to be an empty cow-pen. After Kandan and Chandra had fed and watered the oxen, the three of them found a bed of soft hay a welcome relief and they slept soundly till the morning.

The following morning, it was still dark when Kandan took leave of Chandra and Shubnum. Kandan stooped to touch the feet of both his brother and sister-in-law in the characteristic Indian show of deep respect. The parting was sad and brief. Chandra and Shubnum stood watching silently until the ox-drawn cart with Kandan was absorbed into the darkness.

The farmer had offered to transport Chandra and Shubnum to the train station in Madras, which was a good thirty miles away. This time the cart was drawn by a pair of healthy horses. They made good ground; before long they found themselves at the train station in Madras.

The platform at the station was abuzz with all sorts of human traffic; this was a strange sight for them. Although the sun had risen, there were men, women and children comfortably asleep, on benches and some even on the hard concrete floor, in different parts of the platform and completely oblivious to the robust activity around them. Others pushed and jostled as they made their way through the station. Red buckets of fine grainy sand adorned the walls at strategic points—used for dousing of fires. Uniformed men in turbans shouted reprimands to individuals in long queues at the ticket offices. The atmosphere was permeated with a sulphurous smell of burning coal as a monstrously huge black steam engine gave two short bursts of a horn followed by a long sustained whistle. Chandra and Shubnum watched with curious interest as the engine chugged in, emitting puffs of thick, greyish black smoke and pulling a string of shiny brown coaches. As the windows of the coaches flickered past they realized that the passengers were a diverse group of people; the first two coaches carried Europeans only. Shubnum drew closer to Chandra as she shrunk away from a beggar who jingled some coins in solicitation. The man walked on his knees that were encrusted with constant usage and it had evolved a sole that looked hideously grotesque against his emaciated stick-like limbs. It was not long before they realized that he was just one of many men, women and children who begged all day long; but people went about their business with a cool indifference. For Shubnum and Chandra, who were accustomed to the slow-paced life of a rural community, this was a strange experience. After having gathered some information from others they became aware that they were just two amongst hundreds of others who were on a similar journey with a common destination.

Chandra and Shubnum waited for two hours during which time they found it difficult to secure a stench-free spot where they could rest before boarding the train. The train scheduled for Calcutta announced its arrival with a sustained hoot as it glided in towards the boarding platform. There was a flurry of activity as scores of men and women sprang into action from various positions of repose. Chandra and Shubnum hastily gathered their possessions and made their way towards the coaches. The queue was long and they made slow progress amidst the sounds of voices of men and women as they jostled and pushed. Shubnum had never travelled in a train before, so she stepped into the coach gingerly, looking forward to the experience of a train journey and also feeling relieved at being able to rest. But to their dismay they found that there were not sufficient seats for all the passengers. Many of the seats were removed to accommodate the large numbers. They secured an unoccupied spot on the floor. Here, they spread a blanket on the floor to lend to their comfort and to mark their personal space.

After all passengers had boarded and the locomotive signaled its intention to depart with a prolonged whistle, the engine chugged and transferred its tension to the string of coaches. The train jerked as the metallic couplings adjusted and tensed to overcome its inertia and the coaches glided past the platform, gaining momentum every second. Shubnum stood up to peer through the window as people, animals and carts rushed past at a speed she had not experienced before. Before long the train was puffing merrily along through green verdant hills, across heavy concrete metallic bridges, spanning large rivers and occasionally rushing through tunnels, which plunged the coach into momentary darkness.

The trip was cramped and unpleasant. It had taken two days to reach Calcutta during which time the train had made only three stops. Shubnum was relieved when the train arrived at Calcutta. It did not take them long to realize that everything here was larger and more intense than what they had ever experienced: there were more people; men and women trying to solicit anything from money to food were commonplace; the colonial whites too were a common sight. Though times were hard and life at home in their rural village was austere and difficult, they could not help feeling a deep sense of nostalgia; somehow, reporting to the depot in Calcutta spelt a finality that filled them with anxiety and trepidation.

The depot was not too far away. It was less than a mile from the train station. This was where the potential emigrants were housed temporarily before embarkation. The depot was surrounded by unusually high walls that reminded Chandra of a fortress that housed inmates of a mental institute. Two very large wooden gates shaped like the wings of a butterfly, creaked open under the force of strained effort, by a pair of local Indian men wearing what appeared to be a low ranking military uniform. Chandra and Shubnum, together with scores of other potential emigrants, were ushered into a large courtyard. Two Englishmen stood on a raised platform. One was attired in a civilian outfit while the other was conspicuous in a blue uniform of high-ranking ship's official. His beard, the colour of hay, was immaculately groomed, with his moustache smartly twirled at the ends. The other, a tall, lanky, clean-shaven man, propped a walking stick more as an accessory to his black tailcoat rather than a support for frail limbs. A light skinned turbaned Indian, whose attire reflected a personage of somewhat higher standing than the Indians gathered at the depot, stood a respectful distance from both of them.

The Indians were herded towards the platform. The uniformed Englishman, assumed a more authoritative stance by standing with his legs apart, puffed his chest and clasped his hands behind him, much like a general inspecting his army.

"I am Captain Edgar Simmons, the master of the Belvedere, and will be transporting you across the oceans to Natal," and he turned expectantly towards the turbaned Indian, who intoned in Hindi:

"I am Captain Edgar Simmons and will be taking you to a land of milk and honey."

The Captain continued: "On my right", pointing to the other Englishman, "is Dr Will Cartwright, who will ensure that you are in good health before and during the voyage to Africa."

The Captain looked at the interpreter who responded accordingly.

The Captain waited for his cue to continue and said:

"You will appear before the magistrate who will determine whether you are eligible to emigrate."

The Interpreter responded: *"The magistrate you are going to see will make sure that you will have no problems; he will make sure that all your needs are met."*

The Captain was mildly amused and somewhat intrigued by the mirthful looks of contentment on the chocolate brown faces.

He found it difficult to reconcile the fact that these people would be labouring on a field, thousands of miles from their homes and country and that the passage to Natal was difficult, austere and potentially dangerous and yet they could appear to be contented. It was common knowledge that these people did not leave India as a result of a spirit of enterprise but were driven by poverty.

Even the Captain was ignorant of the fact that the turbaned Indian had a dual role—not only was he the official interpreter but he was also part of the "fifth columns". The "fifth columns" were placed amongst the recruiters to keep the morale of the emigrants high by constantly advertising the merits of emigration and financial prospects that awaited them in the colonies.

The depot was a barracks comprising of a long line of very rudimentary attached enclosures; they were conspicuously empty; there was not a stick of furniture. The emigrants slept on the floor on beds of hay. Their meagre possessions were tied into bundles and placed possessively close to them. Married couples were allowed to be together while males and females were separated as much as possible. However, when there were constraints in floor space, then men and women shared apartments. It was indeed at such times that many unofficial liaisons were formed.

Chandra and Shubnum slept soundly that night. The next day, they found themselves following a queue for medical examination by Dr Will Cartwright, whom the Captain had earlier introduced as the ship's doctor. Shubnum, though diminutive, was a shapely woman with fine, delicate features. She was quite accustomed to attracting the amorous attention of young men.

She had a feeling of unease and awkwardness when she entered Dr Cartwright's examination room. There was a wooden table in a corner behind which Dr Cartwright, clean shaven and immaculately attired in a grey striped suit, sat with his elbows on the table and his chin propped by his interlaced fingers, as he looked pensively above the rim of his glasses. The only other item of furniture was a wooden bed with a very rudimentary covering of a coarse material.

When Shubnum entered he mused, 'Hmmm! You are a fine specimen!'

Although Shubnum did not understand him, she felt uneasy. Intuitively, Shubnum sensed that Dr Cartwright's interest in her went beyond the demands of his profession. He gestured to her to lie on the bed. Shubnum eased herself onto the bed and lay on her back while Dr Cartwright placed a bell-like structure onto her chest with the narrow end making contact with his ears.

"Hmmm!" he mused thoughtfully and shifted his attention to another location on her abdomen. Shubnum was uneasy. She had never been in such close proximity to any other man but Chandra.

If she had thought that, *that* was the greatest state of discomfort and unease that she was going to experience in Dr Cartwright's room, then she was mistaken. Dr Cartwright proceeded to raise Shubnum's sari. She impulsively resisted by tugging her sari down while bending her knees in an attempt to keep her nakedness under cover of her sari.

"I'm a doctor! This is a routine check-up! Don't you want to emigrate?" he asked with a degree of irritation in his voice.

Although she did not understand him well, she gathered that their attempt to emigrate was under threat. She could feel his hand warm and moist, on her thigh, nauseatingly close to the most intimate part of her. She whimpered helplessly and closed her eyes.

Shubnum mentioned nothing of her experience with Cartwright to Chandra. She found herself in a turmoil of moral dilemma and indecision. Although she was not a willing participant in the incident in Dr Cartwright's room, her failure to communicate this information to her husband, had filled her with an intense feeling of guilt. But she knew that divulging such information to her husband would compel Chandra to take steps to restore her honour, which may have dire consequences for their emigration. As painful as it was, she knew that Chandra must never know.

Life at the depot was austere and difficult. Although they were promised many conveniences, the reality at the depot was far from comfortable. The food, which was mostly vegetables, was often bland and did not satisfy the palate of the Indians.

All emigrant Indians could not be accommodated in the apartments in the barracks. Many were herded into a large hall, which was to be their home until they embarked. The large floor space was strewn with individuals, families and couples, with no clear demarcation separating people from each other. In fact, the floor area was shared with an understanding that nobody should invade another's personal space. Quarrels and aggressive arguments over some aspect of encroachment of personal floor space were not uncommon. Shubnum and Chandra took comfort in the fact that this was only temporary and that soon they would be boarding the ship for Africa where life would be more comfortable.

It was this spirit of expectation and hope that had given them the strength and the will to face each new day. The fact that they loved each other dearly was a soothing balm in a world of uncertainty and hardships.

It was the day after they had appeared before the magistrate that Shubnum awoke that morning complaining to Chandra of acute stomach cramps and pain in the area of her abdomen. Both agreed, however, that visiting Dr Cartwright would be detrimental to the success of their emigration. But Shubnum knew — that was not the only reason for not visiting Dr Cartwright.

The frequency of the pains increased. Shubnum frequented the communal latrine and complained of weakness and nausea to Chandra. But it appeared that she was not the only one experiencing these symptoms. The latrines were busier than usual and a strange odour began to permeate the atmosphere in the depot. When Dr Cartwright made an unexpected appearance, to check on the general hygiene, his senses were assaulted by the unmistakable stench of cholera. Cartwright curtailed his inspection and strode back to his wagon with a sense of urgency.

He bent his tall frame into the wagon while gesturing to the wagon driver to make his way to Captain Simmons.

The wagon crunched to a halt on the gravel of the pier not far from a ship with large conspicuous letters spelling out 'Belvedere'.

Cartwright alighted hurriedly and walked briskly towards the gangway of the Belvedere, swinging his stick to the rhythm of his strides. Before long he was on board the Belvedere sitting opposite Captain Simmons in the captain's quarters.

"Simmons! We have a problem! There's cholera amongst the coolie recruits!"

"Are you sure?" Captain Simmons appeared to be nurturing a hope that Simmons may be mistaken.

"Yes, I'm sure!"

"What are the symptoms?" enquired Captain Simmons.

"Watery diarrhea that often contains flecks of whitish material that are the size of pieces of rice and an awful smell!" replied Cartwright with raised and furrowed brows.

"This is highly contagious, Edgar and it is detrimental to ourselves and we could lose many of the recruits long before we reach Africa."

Both men knew the financial implications of this; they were being paid a commission of ten to sixteen shillings per head for their human cargo that reached the destination in good condition.

"What do you suggest, Cartwright?" enquired Simmons.

"Leave as soon as possible! Establish who has contracted the disease and leave them behind!" Simmons appeared to be mulling over the counsel while he held his pipe and nodded his head contemplatively.

Chandra was delighted when he received word that all emigrants would be boarding the Belvedere the following day. But his joy was short lived for he had also heard that all persons who were deemed to be ill would not be permitted to emigrate despite the magistrate having authorized it. But he sought consolation in the fact that Shubnum had not deteriorated to the point where he will not be able to hide her condition from the ship's authorities. Also, the authorities were less stringent with female emigrants than males.

It was 4th October 1860. Shubnum and Chandra awoke to a typical Indian winter. Their meagre possessions fitted into a single sack with draw strings. A disc called the "tin ticket" with a number which allowed them to be identified during the journey, adorned the neck of every recruit. Besides a few rudimentary items such as *dhotis* for the men and saris for the women, every Indian was handed a bowl which they called *lota*. The *lota* was used for ablutions and to drink water.

They stood outside in the courtyard of the depot, together with the others, as instructed. There were three hundred and forty two of them after eight emigrants, men and women, were deemed to be unsuitable to undertake the long voyage. Captain Simmons stood on the platform with Dr Cartwright. With the help of the interpreter, Captain Simmons directed them to walk to the pier and to be in readiness for embarkation onto the Belvedere. While Chandra felt the discomfort of the cold, wintry breeze as it penetrated the thin material of his *kurta*, Shubnum felt its comforting caress against her fever hot body. She was sick—very sick.

She was oblivious to the sounds of men, women and children, shouting, pushing and jostling for positions in the queue. Men shouted instructions to wives that were separated from them in the crowd, mothers reprimanded and restrained bored and frustrated children. Shubnum leaned gently against her husband who placed a comforting hand on her shoulder.

The walk to the Belvedere, though barely half a mile away, was a huge effort for Shubnum. The ship loomed above them— monstrously huge. A large flag, depicting the Royal Banner of England with three lions *passant guardant,* fluttered at the end of a mast. Many of them had never set eyes on a ship before, let alone being so close to one. Now the prospect of boarding one filled many of them with fear.

The gangway that inclined from the ship onto the pier moved gently as the huge ship bobbed continuously with the rhythm of the lapping waters. The emigrants were still boisterous when two junior ship's officers gestured for them to commence boarding. They were required to present their documents to the officers before entering the ship. Many registered stark fear on their faces at the thought of ascending the gangway and took slow, deliberate, fear stricken steps and many of them stopped midway up the gangway, holding the sides rigidly, every time the gangway moved.

Chandra was filled with conflicting thoughts as he waited in the long queue. He felt the compelling urge to escape the austerities of the present, a magnetic attraction towards the promised prospects of the future and yet the sense of foreboding and fear of the unknown, dogged his every thought. And amidst all this, the thought of Shubnum being ill, clouded his mind and worried him in no small measure.

·········ᴇᴇᴇ◇◇◇ᴇᴇᴇ·········

The ship's environment was strange to all of them. The feeling of unsteadiness emanating from the gentle tilt and sway of the ship evoked interesting responses; the children thought it was fun. Many were intrigued and others viewed it with trepidation. But it was not long before none of them paid any heed to it.

They were shown to their quarters below the deck. Single men and women were placed on either end of the ship while married couples and children were accommodated in the middle.

Chandra and Shubnum found themselves in an apartment no larger than a small cow pen—just large enough to accommodate a bunk-bed. Shubnum was only too pleased to collapse onto the lower bed. Her condition had deteriorated but she continued to project an image of all being well lest the master of the ship discovered that she was very ill.

Captain Simmons appeared to be all over the ship, shouting orders to his crew. After he was satisfied that all had boarded, he ordered the anchor to be raised and the Belvedere creaked and strained as it glided out of the Port of Calcutta with its cargo of human beings.

Despite the anxieties, the cramped and unhygienic conditions, the good weather with blue skies and a gentle breeze, buoyed the spirits of the Indians. They engaged in boxing and wrestling as entertainment. Even the crew found it entertaining. Paruk, a bald headed Indian with a simian look and a short neck, broad shoulders and massive arms, was a favourite both in boxing and wrestling. The hair Paruk lacked on his head, sprouted profusely on the rest of his body. He had a reputation for being unbeaten. Often the men would form a ring on the deck and the pugilists would occupy the centre. Wagers were taken in gold or rupees. On this day, Paruk occupied the centre but there was no adversary. A few knew Chandra as an athlete and a formidable adversary in boxing.

"*Bhaiya!*" someone called out from the crowd, referring to Chandra, "*Show this gorilla who's the champ!*"

Chandra ignored the man. Paruk sniggered, "*Get a real man to face me!*" Chandra now became the focus of unwanted attention. He felt someone shove him and found himself at the middle of the ring, and the crowd roared in appreciation. Paruk, bent low, balled his fists and stiffened his body — ready to strike or defend. Chandra was taller, younger and clearly an athlete. But Chandra knew that Paruk was no easy adversary and he must fight this man intelligently; he should keep a distance since he was taller. Paruk tried to close in to enjoy the advantage of a shorter reach but Chandra danced back nimbly. Chandra feigned a blow to the head. Paruk raised his arm to effect a block and Chandra found his opening. His right arm shot out through the gap. He made a full-blooded impact with a bone-shattering effect on Paruk's nose. Paruk was momentarily dazed and looked surprised as blood oozed through his nostrils. He grunted with anger as he charged with a right hook at Chandra's head. Chandra stepped aside skilfully and let his right arm find the soft of his solar-plexus. Paruk bent over in pain and picked up his arm, gesturing for Chandra to stop.

Shubnum was asleep when Chandra saw her again. She awoke later in the night and vomited several times into a bucket and had to be helped to make her way to the ship's latrine. In the days that followed, she became increasingly weak. The well-moulded healthy look was fast disappearing. Her skin was losing its elasticity. Chandra suggested that she sees the ship's doctor. Shubnum protested vehemently but she was weak. Chandra knew that she was seriously ill. One morning he decided to ignore her protests and went in search of Dr Cartwright.

Dr Cartwright's expression showed serious concern on examining Shubnum. He held her skin on the abdomen between his forefinger and thumb and pinched gently. It left a depression very much like pinching soft clay.

"She is extremely dehydrated!" he said, looking at Chandra with furrowed brows while he picked up her hands to scrutinize her fingers which appeared shriveled and bony like the fingers of one who has been engaging in excessive washing.

It was patently evident that Dr Cartwright was not in any position to assure Shubnum or Chandra of relief, either immediately or long term. He dissolved a pinch of salt in a glass of water, which he handed to Chandra to administer more as a perfunctory gesture rather than a genuine intent to cure. He was not pleased for all the symptoms that Shubnum displayed shouted out 'cholera'. "How did she slip through?" he thought. He was worried. Given that cholera was easily communicable, this could spell disaster — he was extremely concerned about the monetary implications. The design of the ship was such that the Indians were close and cramped. Something had to be done to stop the spread of the disease — she had to be isolated!

They were subsequently removed to an isolated part of the ship. It was more comfortable and spacious. But Shubnum's condition continued to deteriorate. They were already ten days out at sea.

Her cheeks had sunk in and her skin appeared to have been pulled taut over the bones of her face. The once healthy mounds of her breasts looked diminished and wrinkled like oversized dried prunes. Her fingers looked gnarled and arthritic, like she had aged overnight.

Chandra was by her side all the time. She whimpered continuously and at times she was delirious. She spoke of her childhood in her delirium and recalled the many happy moments she had enjoyed with her siblings. At times she would giggle coquettishly and call for Chandra—and he was always there. But on this day she was wide-awake. Her eyes reflected a spirit of the days of fun, love and laughter.

"Chandra!" her voice was almost a whisper. *"Come closer!"*

He bent over her lovingly.

"You know that I cannot complete this voyage!" She clasped his hand desperately.

"We shall reach Africa together!" he said but the lump in his throat betrayed his attempt at optimism.

"Listen to me! My voyage is different from yours. Where I go you cannot follow. I go alone!"

"No don't say that!" he placed his finger on her lips to hush her.

"I love you!" he said. *"Don't leave me!"*

"They are waiting for me!" she turned to look at the side.

"Who is waiting for you?" he asked curiously.

"The angels! Don't you see them?" and she pointed feebly to the side of the bed.

"I have to go! They are beckoning me!" she whispered.

Tears welled up in his eyes and dribbled down his cheek as he buried his face against her frail body and sobbed uncontrollably.

Of the three hundred and forty two men, women and children who had boarded the Belvedere at the Port of Calcutta on 4 October 1860, three hundred and thirteen arrived alive at the Port of Good Hope, on 26th November 1860. At the time of their arrival the Zulus were locked in battle with the British and their arrival was inauspicious. The attitude and the perceptions of the Colonial British were aptly captured by John Robinson, in an article in the Natal *Mercury*.

> *A very remarkable scene was the landing of the first batch of Indian indentured labourers and one well worth remembrance and record. Most of the spectators who were present had been led to expect a lot of dried up, vapid, and sleepy-looking anatomies. They were agreeably disappointed. The swarthy hordes came pouring out of the boat's hold, laughing, jabbering, and staring about them with a very well satisfied expression of self complacency on their faces . . . A queer, comical, foreign-looking, very oriental-like crowd. The men, with their huge muslin turbans, bare scraggy skin-bones, and coloured garments; the women with their flashing eyes, long disheveled pitchy hair, with their half covered, well-formed figures and their keen inquisitive glances; the children with their meager, intelligent, cute and humorous countenances mounted on bodies of inconceivable fragility, were all evidently beings of a different race and kind to any we have yet seen . . . . Master coolie seemed to make himself quite at home, and was not in the least disconcerted by the novelty of the situation . . . . The boats seemed to disgorge an endless stream of living cargo-Pariahs, Christians, Malabars, and Mohommedans . . . .*

Many had not eaten a good meal in three months. Chandra, and many others like him refused to eat the cured pork and beef, which were offered on the ship; bad light, poor ventilation and lack of fresh water forced many to succumb to the dreaded cholera. Their relief at arriving at their destination, however, was short lived. The ship was placed in quarantine on arrival on the instructions of the Health Officer. The English Colonists were in stark fear of infection and they also resented the extra costs incurred by the disease. The clothing and bedding of all passengers were burnt and replaced. Besides the mental and emotional turmoil of losing members of the family to the dreaded disease, they were exhausted and spiritually drained. They were housed temporarily in lazarettos and stuffy tents. Many more died while they awaited their recovery. During this time Chandra felt the loss of Shubnum intensely. His mind reeled with the memories of her.

She was twenty years old and he, twenty-four, when the parents of both Chandra and Shubnum arranged to meet without their knowledge. This was a common practice in India and a source of great anxiety to the potential victims of the bridal pact. But in the case of Chandra and Shubnum, their anxieties were unfounded; she was slim, attractive and intelligent and he—a strong, sturdy young man who showed all signs of growing into a patriarch with many, many off-springs. That was five years ago. It was unfortunate that Shubnum bore him no children—this was a source of anxiety for both of them—for the family of Chandra made no effort to hide their extreme dissatisfaction. Shubnum cried. She always cried. But she sought refuge in the fact that her husband was a kind and loving soul. Often, they would steal away to sit beneath their favorite tamarind tree and listen to the stream gurgling and whispering over the boulders made smooth by centuries of erosion. They laughed, teased and loved below the tamarind tree.

After a fortnight of quarantine, they were allowed to leave the Belvedere. Chandra stepped gingerly onto the wooden trellis of the ship's gangway. His eyes were brimming with tears—he did not even hear the pop and creak of the wooden cross-timbers of the gangway as the huge steamer bobbed and dipped with the gentle rise and fall of the waves; the thought of Shubnum, wrapped in the ship's sack, fastened at the neck and ankles and jettisoned into the cold, murky depths of the Indian Ocean, brought on a deluge of tears he could not control. He felt somewhat strange walking on the grey shale surface of the pier after spending almost ninety days at sea. The land appeared strange and the people even stranger.

The golden orb of the sun was already sinking in the horizon, casting luminous red panels of light across the western sky. This is the time that Kandan would be herding the bulls and Lutchmee, the only cow, into the pen. Chandra could almost hear the tinkle of the bells amidst the mooing of the silhouetted cattle as they made their way home. His father, would be sitting on the paint flaked bench, in the crude open porch of the thatch roofed farmhouse, lazily swatting flies. Chandra was awoken suddenly from his reverie by the booming horn of an English vessel entering the harbour, with its Union Jack dancing jauntily in the breeze. Tears snaked down his chaffed, dry, chocolate-brown face; he had not shaved for several days and he looked unkempt. He joined his group of countrymen who had gathered before a rather, tall, burly Englishman who boomed out something incomprehensible to the group. Chandra noticed his bushy golden moustache, which was smartly twirled at the edges. Next to him was a short Indian man, sporting a white traditional Indian *kurta* with a black evening coat, similar to those worn by English gentlemen—an odd combination. The Englishman continued to address the group of Indian labourers and at intervals stopped to look at the Indian next to him, who intoned in Hindi. Chandra barely listened but managed to elicit that they would be transported to their sleeping quarters and their respective farms the following morning. His heart was thumping against his chest and his eardrums were pounding and it was not with excitement—his anxiety and trepidation knew no bounds.

He followed the crowd to a large horse-drawn cart, one of many, which was ready and waiting. They were divided into groups of twenty and Chandra's group was accommodated in the large cart. The driver, a dark skinned man with peppercorn hair, the likes of whom Chandra had never seen before, cracked his whip and the cart trundled off; within a few minutes he could just barely make out the silhouetted figures going about their business at the pier, which was fast receding from sight. The metal rims of the cart crunched and gritted along the gravel road with the driver yelling in a strange dialect to keep the horse on track. Before long, the darkness had overtaken them. They travelled silently, save for an occasional deep cough from Panday, one of the emigrants, who had taken ill on the ship.

When Chandra first heard that, in South Africa, gold nuggets were strewn in the streets like stones, he was sceptical. But the reports were coming in more frequently and from sources that he had reason neither to disbelieve nor doubt; gold in India had always held pride of place in every home. The lure of gold and the opportunity to change one's social status with money was not to be ignored. Many braved the hardships and austerities of the long journey, driven by the hope of a better future.

It was not only the attraction of the prospects across the seas that had lured the Indians in their multitudes but also the pressures from the land of their birth; poverty and the harsh living conditions in India, aggravated by drought, disease and famine have strengthened their resolve to leave India.

Chandra's deep contemplation was interrupted by the sudden jerk of the cart when it stopped. They had travelled along a wide boulevard, lined on either side by tall trees with spreading luscious foliage. It was a cloudless night and the myriad of stars that glittered in the dark sky made him realize that it was much like *Bharat*; a few very bright stars were spread across a nebulous cluster that looked like tiny grains of sparkling sand. A glacial cold breeze nipped occasionally at the exposed parts of their bodies. Most of the labourers, including Chandra, were accustomed to the warm nights of *Bharat*, where turning in for the night, was an informal arrangement; it was not unusual to lie out in the open porch or even outside to sleep the whole night.

He held on tightly to his sack which contained his only possessions, as they were herded into a wood and iron structure. Many of them had to dip their heads in order to go through the small entrance. They found themselves in a shed, where an oil lamp burned dimly in a corner, throwing large, grotesque, caricatured shadows across the mud floor. About fifty paces from them, several cows with rheumy eyes, turned their heads curiously and lazily to view the new visitors and room-mates. The strong smell of dung did not offend them; they had been subjected to worse in the ship's tiny cabins. Chandra recalled with an involuntary shudder the putrid stench of death, disease, faeces and vomit in the confined spaces of the cabins. They had not been allowed onto the deck without the explicit permission of the captain, something which was almost impossible to get, given the language constraints and access to the captain. Chandra could not shake off the thought of Shubnum lying in the watery grave of the Indian Ocean—it tore at his heart. He was still deep in thought and recalled in vivid detail the gloominess, the unwholesomely cold and squalid conditions aboard the Belvedere, which Shubnum was so terrified of, when the silence was broken by a nasally voice, which jarred him.

"You will be transported tomorrow to your work stations, tonight, you will rest and sleep and tomorrow you shall work."

When Chandra opened his eyes, with his head somewhat bowed, he noticed a pair of shiny, brown leather riding boots. The occupant of the boots was a rather large Englishman. He appeared to have come from riding for he clasped a folded riding whip close to his chest as he spoke.

"I am Croft—Harold Croft. But to you I am your master! You are clearly beings of a race different to any kind we have yet seen in Natal. I have been told that you coolies can steal a bull under an Englishman's nose. Do not give me any reason to flog you. You have been shipped here at great cost to ourselves. Do an honest day's job and you will be compensated. I shall not tolerate malingering and laziness."

He did not seem to be concerned about the fact that they understood very little or nothing of what he said but he appeared to be satisfying an intrinsic urge to stamp his authority as the master. His large twirled golden moustache twitched and bristled like the fur on the back of an angry cat as he spoke.

They stood in grim silence, clutching their possessions. The only other sound besides the voice of the Englishman was the incessant coughing of Panday, a recruit from Bombay, who had taken ill during the voyage. Although they understood very little of what was said, they knew that it was not pleasant. Croft clasped his whip under his left arm, thrust his hands into his pocket, turned on the ball of his feet and strode out. The grim and stony silence that followed was broken by the unceasing coughing of Panday.

Their sleep broke with the sounds of the metallic clunk of chain against padlock as the herd—boy prepared to open the large wooden gate of the shed to let out the cattle. Chandra stretched and yawned. Next to him Panday appeared to be fast asleep.

He reached out towards Panday, held his shoulder and shook him. "*Get up!*" he said in Hindi. But Panday's lifeless body just flopped. His body fluid trickled obscenely from the nostril taking the slant of his head. Chandra pulled his hand away impulsively. Chapu, whose frosted brows and silvery fringe of hair qualified him to be the most knowledgeable and experienced in such matters as death and dying and the associated traditions and customs, knelt beside Panday's still form and placed the fingers of his right hand on Panday's neck below his left ear. Observing no sign of life he placed his ear on Panday's chest to confirm his diagnosis. There was a grim silence in the shed before Chapu punctuated it with, *"He's gone!"* Just then the door creaked as Croft opened the little side entrance and bent his way in. His gaze fell on Panday's body immediately.

"Now, what do we have here?" he said as he strode up to Panday's lifeless body.

"He is either a lazy Indian or a dead Indian!" he exclaimed as he started to shove and push the corpse with his foot in an attempt to establish its status. While the group watched in horror and disbelief at the Englishman's insensitivity and total lack of respect, Shiraz, an unusually large Indian, lumbered up to Croft from the rear and held the Englishman firmly at the scruff of his neck with his left hand and hooked the fingers of his right hand at the seat of his breeches. Croft was propelled head first into a large patty of fresh dung that the cattle had recently deposited. The wind was knocked out of Croft, whose nose and mouth were firmly ensconced in the fresh, warm dung. He gulped, involuntarily sucking in the redolent dung, much to his horror.

He recovered quickly. He used his right hand to squeeze the mess from his forehead down to his chin. His once pale face appeared crimson beneath the specks of green still stuck in his bearded face as he stormed out. They all knew that Croft would be back.

Shiraz was a Muslim. His large frame sported a girth, which was amply accentuated by a colourful, oriental shawl tied around his waist. He was a full head taller than most Indian men. He sported a full beard with streaks of early greying that somehow gave him a distinguished look. Shiraz's immense strength was common knowledge; he picked up Panday's body and carried him outside. The sun was already a good distance in the sky; Shiraz placed the body on a carpet of grass. Already metallic green flies buzzed incessantly around the corpse, settling on the face and crawling in and out of the nostrils. Most of the dead in India were cremated in an open pyre. This was preceded by a host of rituals that took several hours. But preparing the pyre was a long and arduous task. This, clearly, was not possible here—a new country with strange people with even stranger customs and traditions. They had seen many of their loved ones, friends and acquaintances, who had succumbed to the dreaded cholera and other ailments, unceremoniously dropped from the ship's deck into the green and murky depths of the Indian Ocean. Somehow this had helped to fortify them against the sensitivities of deviations from accustomed traditions and rituals. It was Chandra who spoke first.

"Brothers!" He addressed the small group of men only. The women were accustomed to being excluded from important decisions.

"We are far away from home. We have gone through much in our voyage from Bharat. I myself have seen the love of my life, wrapped in a sack and thrown overboard. The ocean is her grave. The feringhees man will not allow us to observe the necessary customs and rituals and we all know that he will be back. God knows what we should expect. We can only pray to the Lord for mercy. We must bury him as soon as possible, before he returns." The mood was solemn.

One of the indigenous labourers, a native with grey peppercorn hair, had identified a spot, twenty minutes of walking distance into the thick undergrowth where farm labourers were usually buried. Panday's body was placed on a sack. Four men held each corner of the material as they bore the corpse to the burial site. There was a solemn silence until one of the women broke into a song; the mellifluous, flutelike sound of the voice added to the solemnity of the occasion. Panday was buried that day, ten thousand miles away from home and family, amidst tears, whispers and chanting.

The extraordinary action, earlier, of Shiraz against Croft, was still uppermost in the minds of all the Indians. While some thought of it as being extremely bold, others thought it was foolhardy and still others lauded it as a natural action from one who has the blood of a warrior coursing through him. Although the Indians were from a land that had been colonized by the British, who clearly considered themselves as a superior, dominant race, the relationship between the British and the Indians was by no means akin to master and slave and the Indians were therefore, not accustomed to it. Shiraz never perceived Croft as a master who, like all masters, were considered to be insulated from aggression or offence from servants and slaves. So Shiraz perceived his action as obligatory—as that of a man who was offended by the lack of respect from another towards his fellow man.

When the little crowd returned to the farmstead, Croft was there, waiting with a double-barreled shotgun tucked firmly under his right arm; he was flanked by two men, one taller and the other a shade shorter. The taller man had coils of rope slung around his left shoulder while the other carried a pail of what appeared to be water. But this was a pail of concentrated salt solution. Although Croft was silent, his intentions were clear. Save for an almost imperceptible nod from him, as a signal for the man with the rope to act, there was no communication. The atmosphere was tense with fear and anxiety.

Although, men and women surrounded Shiraz, to insulate and protect him from Croft's aggression, his large frame did little to give him refuge—he towered above the rest. Little blisters of perspiration pimpled his forehead. Despite his stark fear, he pushed gently through the group, until he stood facing the men. Croft immediately leveled his shotgun, which was now aimed at

Shiraz's broad chest. The others in the group slowly slunk away to the sides. Shiraz extended his arms forward in a mute invitation of surrender. The man unslung the rope as he walked towards him. He wasted no time in having Shiraz's hands tightly bound. About fifty paces away, stood a large tree with spreading foliage. The rope was slung over an overhanging branch. As the man pulled at the rope, Shiraz's arms stretched until he could feel the rope biting into his wrist. The loose end of the rope was then tied around a lower branch.

Croft stepped up to Shiraz from the rear and hooked his fingers into the collar of his loose fitting garment and ripped it down to the waist; the garment lay in tattered rags at his feet. Layers of fat around his large girth folded over, looking like gills of a large fish; most of the other Indians were darker skinned, lean and gaunt. Shiraz was different. Croft surveyed the group of Indians with a cynical sneer, placed the shotgun against the bole of a tree and armed himself with a whip, which he had tucked away in his breeches.

The whip whistled as it snaked above his head, while he twirled it with the skill of a circus lion handler, and then lunged forward while extending his whip arm. The whip cracked and tore into Shiraz's meaty back. His flesh opened exposing the fatty layer beneath. Shiraz winced but did not utter a sound. Croft continued assaulting his back. By this time, the low murmur that started amongst the group increased until the women wailed and men let out a string of profanities in Hindi and Tamil, imploring Croft to stop. Shiraz's body was a mess of bloody streaks. He was barely conscious and started to sag at the knees, while the rope tensed, causing the branch to bow. The man with the pail stepped forward and emptied the contents onto Shiraz's open wounds. But Shiraz was beyond the point of sensing any further pain. The Indian labourers were by this time, extremely agitated. While the women wailed, the men continued to utter expletives with clenched fists; they needed just the tiniest of prod to unleash their pent up aggression. Croft sensed this and quickly grabbed the shotgun, which was leaning against the bole of the tree. He held it comfortably with his right arm while the muzzle rested on the crook of his left arm. He pointed it menacingly towards the frenzied group of Indians. Under threat of being shot, the Indians fell silent. Chandra, broke away from the group and with measured and defiant steps made his way towards the slumped figure of Shiraz. He loosened the rope from around the tree. By this time Ananda, a middle-aged Indian from the deep south of India had Shiraz resting on his shoulder to soften his landing when the rope was released.

The incident was not reported to the magistrate, the only accessible route to relevant authorities to seek redress for any form of injustice. In a robust debate at a little gathering under a tree, the following afternoon, most, including Chandra, were of the firm view that reporting the assault on Shiraz would not serve any purpose; in fact, it might implicate Shiraz more than it would Croft, given the fact that it was Shiraz who had humiliated Croft initially and Croft had reacted like any master would. Such incidents were complicated and weighed heavily against the Indians; in the absence of a skilled and competent interpreter and given the deep prejudices held by magistrates and judges, the Indians knew that that they were bound to lose even though they had solid, substantial evidence.

Chandra and three others, two men and a woman were ordered by Croft to walk to a farm in Ifafa, to report to John Bennet, their new master. They walked for many miles and many hours. The road was flanked by sugar cane plantations on either side. At times, the height of the cane reached higher than their heads and in some places it diminished to half the size; then they were able to see the refreshing blue of the ocean; they could see the frothy white waves chasing each other to the shore and for a moment they were not aware of their thirst, and the pain in their limbs. The sun had climbed only a short distance in the eastern horizon and already they could feel the heat and the discomfort. They had walked long enough for the sun to be almost directly above them but the end was not in sight. Their bare feet were chapped and bruised. Rivulets of sweat snaked their way down the sides of their faces. At intervals they took the end of their *caftans* and mopped themselves. The woman, known as Meena, was dark skinned with jet-black hair, which was tied in a single plait. She was a little over five feet tall; although she looked emaciated and her cheekbones protruded beneath her taut skin, her eyes reflected a spirit of having seen better days. Her clothes were nothing more than a length of thin, coarse material, which was once white, awkwardly wrapped around her, one end of which was thrown over her shoulder to cover her nakedness. Just when she thought that she could walk no more, they spotted a white farmhouse about half a mile away. Thin wisps of smoke curled up from the chimney. They plodded on with renewed strength.

They were greeted by the incessant barking of dogs. They limped on painfully until they reached a terraced pathway that led to a spacious open patio with a thatched roof. The barking attracted the attention of a large black buxom woman, who addressed them in a language they did not understand. An English woman, with brown curly locks falling lazily around her shoulder, stepped daintily onto the patio. On seeing her, the Indians steepled their palms in their characteristic manner of greeting and display of deep respect. To Chandra, Claudia Bennet was a goddess. She broke into a smile that revealed two hollow dimples; her loose flowing dress draped softly over the contours of her body.

"They look awfully tired and exhausted. Poor devils! Tembi!" she called out.

"I am sure they are famished. Give them something to eat and drink."

While the other two took only a casual interest in the English woman, Chandra was mesmerized by this beautiful creature. He hunched slightly at the shoulder in a reverential bow and his palms were clasped before him, respectfully.

They sat on a rock in a shade of a large spreading jacaranda tree. The water from the brown porcelain mug was refreshing. Tembi waddled over with three large apples clasped comfortably in her large palms. The sound of galloping horses was distinctive in the quiet of the day. They turned simultaneously towards the direction of the sound. Two riders came into focus amidst a cloud of dust. As they drew closer, the man on the large brown stallion brought his horse to a trot and stopped beside the group. The other, a younger man, in his twenties galloped away leaving a trail of dust behind him.

The older, was a large man, with close-cropped dark brown hair. A thick mat of brown, untrimmed beard hid his round face. His long moustache almost covered his lips and when he spoke it appeared like a sound emanating from a mop of hair. His large frame straddled the horse as if horse and rider were one.

"So the coolies have finally arrived!" he exclaimed, as he surveyed the group thoughtfully.

"I have paid good money for you and you have already lost many hours of working time. The cane is ready to be harvested; in fact, it ought to have been done a week ago. We have lost a lot of time."

He squinted at the sun which was almost directly overhead, to get an estimate of the time.

"The tools are in the shed!" He pointed at a wood and iron structure about fifty yards away.

"You still have a good six hours of daylight left! Now get going!"

The British occupation of India had equipped some of the Indians with a smattering of English. Many viewed it as the language of the oppressors and therefore acquired it only if circumstances had thrust it upon them. English was truly a foreign tongue to these indentured labourers. If they understood anything, it would have been the general body language and tone and this white man was by no means friendly. On hearing the sound of the galloping horses, Tembi had already scurried away awkwardly towards the cottage as she had no intention of being anywhere near the boss, whose vile temperament was common knowledge to the entire household. The Indians did not move but looked at him in silent confusion.

Bennet slid down from his saddle. Chandra stood up still clutching the apple and staring blankly at him, having understood very little. Suddenly, Bennet lashed out with the open palm of his hand at Chandra's face. The sudden explosion of air against his eardrums deafened him momentarily and his head reeled with dizziness. Meena and the two male labourers backed away hastily. Chandra's rage knew no bounds. But he remembered the fate of Shiraz; the memory of Shiraz's limp body mingled graphically with the crimson mess of torn flesh and tattered garments. He clenched his fists and stiffened his body in a concerted effort to restrain himself from retaliating. Claudia, who observed the incident through the kitchen window, came running, clutching her skirt so that it would not sweep the ground, and placed herself strategically between her husband and Chandra, lest he unleashed another assault on the Indian.

"*That* was not necessary!" she hissed.

"Can you not see that they do not understand you?" She glowered at him and made no attempt to hide her rage. Bennet was furious; he felt belittled and his ego was being battered and bruised but he knew better than to challenge his wife. In a valiant attempt to show his authority and to salvage his damaged ego he pointed to the field and said, "The field is there, now get to work!" But there was an almost imperceptible tremble in his finger as he pointed to the field.

Skinny, emaciated dark skinned men in colourful dhotis and turbans spotted the green field. They chatted nonchalantly as they hacked through the cane, leaving distinctive boundaries between the cut and the uncut cane. Dimunitive, dark skinned women hiding their nakedness in loose fitting saris toiled silently under the burning midday sun. Meena toiled mechanically— her thoughts were far away, over the oceans. The thought of her sisters and the other girls in the village making their way with empty water pots, clasped under their arms, to the river to collect drinking water made her smile; the many stories they exchanged of young men and relationships, while they sat on rounded boulders on the river's edge, made her long for home. Raju, the cowherd had taken a fancy to her. But he was only a cowherd—although she liked the attention and he was not bad looking. When she left, she had not told anyone. She was desperate to escape the deep poverty; she was one of six children and the conditions were not getting any better. She knew that she was caught in an inextricable cycle of poverty and the cruel and heinous caste system; as long as she stayed In India she would always be a low-caste Indian fit only for the most menial of tasks. But the passage to Africa promised a life of prosperity and hope.

She did not hear the almost imperceptible hiss as she cleared the cut cane with her bare hands. As she scooped the bundle, coil upon coil of a scaly, olive green menace had already drawn its head back—the snake was poised and tensed, like a drawn bow, and ready to strike. She stared in mute terror. The momentum of the strike caused it to uncoil and reach almost its complete length; the white needle like fangs looked conspicuous against the black linings of the mouth; its teeth buried deep on the side of her neck while the soft scaly body dangled obscenely against her, writhing in a grotesque manoeuvre to obtain purchase to release itself. There was a muffled cry from Meena as she clawed and pushed erratically to rid herself of the loathsome creature. As it fell to the ground, it struck again—this time on her foot. The snake uncoiled and slithered away, dragging its soft, slack body over the undulating mound of earth, into the cane field.

Meena fell to the ground, clasping the side of her neck. Her eye balls were rolled up, showing the white of her eyes while the dark brown iris appeared like eclipsed half-moons below her upper eyelids. As she gasped for air, bubbles of spittle frothed at the side of her mouth. Marie, a fellow labourer, was the first to reach Meena. It took him a few moments to realize that he needed to get help. He hobbled away on his spindly legs towards the farmhouse, which was a good three hundred yards away.

John Bennet was at the table sipping and relishing a cup of tea from an enamel cup when he saw Marie gesticulating earnestly to catch his attention. When Bennet recognized that Marie was trying to communicate that something has happened and that he was required, it was already ten minutes at least since Meena had been bitten. Claudia Bennet, on hearing that something was amiss, appeared on the patio. "Hurry!" she said, clearly concerned, "I think someone has been bitten by a snake!" While John Bennet made his way towards the field, Claudia ordered her son Claude, who had been catching up on his midday snooze, to run to the field to render any form of assistance.

Meena was quite still when Bennet reached her. Her eyes stared vacantly into space. Spittle had dribbled down her chin and dried, leaving a whitish trace. Bennet held her left hand with his fingers on the inner side of her wrist to establish any palpitations of the pulse. After a few seconds he declared, "I think she is dead!" He ordered two men to carry her to the cottage. They placed her respectfully on a straw mat in the wood and iron shed. John Bennet requested his son to ride into the village to summon the doctor. It was almost three hours later when Dr Smith arrived at the farmstead. Within a minute he pronounced her dead.

Clearly Caudia Bennet had won the hearts of the Indians. It was through her that they had been allowed not only to finish the day early but also to use the horse-drawn cart to transport Meena's corpse to the barracks. They tried to observe as much of the ceremonial rites as possible and Meena was buried.

This did little for their morale and confidence. Chandra was overcome by a deep sense of nostalgia. This was not a land of milk and honey as was promised. Alone in his quarters in the barracks, his mind played out the events of the past few days. His intense anger at Bennet's insensitivity and his gratuitous show of aggression worried him in no small measure. It was at these times that he felt the absence of Shubnum the most and it was at times like these that he regretted having left his family and India. His hands trembled as he picked up the end of his *caftan* to dab the tears from his eyes.

Chandra's quarters in the barracks, a long wood and iron structure with several little enclosures, was almost dark, save for a panel of light from a single window, just large enough to pop one's head through. The only items of furniture were a crude wooden table and pair of matching chairs. A faint smell of cow dung permeated the air. Earlier that day, Baigum, a female indentured labourer in her mid-twenties, had come in with a bucket full of cow dung which she had offered to lay on the floor of his quarters, much like paving a floor with cement; this was temporary and had to be done at least once a week. Chandra lay on his straw bed, propped on his elbows, watching Baigum spread the dung.

Baigum was attractive — she reminded him of Shubnum. She was unusual for an indentured labourer; she could almost be described as voluptuous. Although her black hair was unkempt and hung loosely around her shoulders it did not diminish her beauty. Her face broke into a pair of mysterious dimples on her cheeks at the slightest smile. With her loose fitting sari rucked up above her knees, she painstakingly layered the patties of cow dung and pounded it firmly into the ground until it produced a fairly level and smooth surface. But Chandra watched with only a casual interest. Occasionally, she would stop to pick up the end of her sari to mop her face and smile at him. But he was still too deeply in love with Shubnum to even notice that Baigum was attracted to him.

It was a Saturday. Nobody worked during week-ends. The Indians looked forward to this; during this time men and women would engage in some form of entertainment; wrestling between men was popular and very often resulted in hilarious consequences. But the one event that embraced entertainment, spiritual growth and a satisfaction of a religious obligation, was gathering at the village temple; this usually took place on a Saturday evening.

The pounding of drums from the village temple attracted his attention. The sweet, lilting sound of a flute wafted lazily to the far ends of the barracks. Men, like moles, peeked out of their doors and then made their way towards the temple. Chandra slipped on his sandals and followed the sound. Baigum was disappointed but she continued faithfully to complete the layering of the dung.

Chandra found the gathering of all the village folk at the temple and the idle chatter, together with the multitude of cultural events, entertaining and a welcome relief from the backbreaking work during the week. On this night, men with painted faces danced to the beat of drums while miming a sketch; some men were adorned in women's garb to fit the role of females. The crowd loved every moment and found it hilariously funny. Chandra too, found himself caught in the wave of fun and gaiety.

When he returned to his quarters later that night, Baigum was asleep on the floor on a straw mat. While he was surprised at her presence, he realized for the first time just how beautiful she was. In the dim light of the oil lamp, her features took on a softness he had never noticed before; a wisp of dark curl of her hair adorned her forehead like a piece of jewelry. He watched her chest rise and fall with every breath and he felt a closeness he had not felt before but his feelings were not without a tinge of guilt—this being the first time he had felt any affection for a woman since Shubnum. He covered her gently with a frayed grey blanket and retired to bed.

It was Monday and Chandra awoke early. It was still dark outside. He always started his day early: earlier than the stipulated time of six 'o clock—especially after John Bennet had informed them that he would be taking an audit of the number of bales of cane harvested per labourer with the possible intention of punishing the underperformer. While there was no indication of a reward for workers who produced a high yield, Chandra nurtured a hope that Bennet would use productivity to appoint a *sirdar*. He therefore left at least an hour before the others to ensure that his harvest surpassed that of everybody else. Baigum was trying to get the coal stove going. Although he felt awkward at her being there, he could not bring himself to say anything lest he disturbed the comfortable ease with which she went about her business in the kitchen. The smoke made his eyes smart. It was not long before the room was filled with a glowing warmth. Baigum offered him a cup of tea made from fresh cow's milk. He always loved his tea. He gulped it down with a relish and left the warmth of the room for the chill of the cold wintry morning.

He followed the narrow footpath where the dew laden slender leaves of the stunted shrubs whipped uncomfortably against his bare limbs. The cold breeze numbed his ear lobes and the tip of his nose. He wrapped his hands with the ends of his caftan and walked with a slight slouch as if that would ease the cold. His oversize shoes that were given to him by one of the white *sahibs* felt uncomfortable as he wound his way up the narrow path that led past Bennet's cottage. The dim light of the moon cast ghostly images along the way. In a vain attempt to protect his ears, he tried to cover his head with the caftan as the cold sting of the icy breeze numbed his face. Myriads of stars were splashed across the sky and the silhouetted outline of Bennet's cottage protruded out of the dark horizon. As he neared the house, he noticed the dim light of the lamp against the curtains. The luminosity of the oil lamp in Bennet's bedroom contrasted starkly against the shadowy silhouette of the rest of the house. But something was different. The movement of the figures against the curtain was unusually erratic and quick. He recognised the petite outline of a woman, whom he presumed was Claudia Bennet; the shadowy figure of a bigger, taller person morphed with that of the female figure. He instinctively felt a sense of unease and foreboding. The silence of the morning was broken by a piercing but strangled cry, just for a moment, and then the figures disappeared from view. He crouched behind a shrub, not knowing what to do. Should he approach the house? There could be serious trouble in the Bennet household. He lay low, pondering what would be the appropriate action given the fact that he was an Indian labourer and the perceived problem was within the confines of his employer's private residence. His attempt at offering assistance could very well be construed as intrusion and this could be detrimental to his dream of becoming a *sirdar*. Minutes ticked by as he continued to crouch behind the shrub. On the other hand, he could be missing an opportunity to feature as a hero; even the ill-tempered *Sahib* would be obliged to reward him and what better way than to have him appointed as a *sirdar*. Even Mrs Bennet would look favourably upon him. He was lost in his thoughts when the silence was interrupted by the clack and clatter of a door bolt being opened. A man stepped out with a lantern held above his head. The circle of light cast down by the lantern danced to the rhythm of the steps as the man made his way to the stable. Chandra recognised the broad brimmed hat of John Bennet. The shuffling gait as he made his way to the stables was unmistakeably the *sahib*. Within a few minutes Bennet galloped away leaving a trail of dust in the dim moonlight. Despite the cold, Chandra felt beads of perspiration pimpling his forehead and he was breathing heavily. But he felt a sense of relief — the problem could be no more than a quarrel between a husband and his wife. In any event, the son, Claude was also there and Chandra was of the firm view that it was not his place to become embroiled, in his employer's private affairs, at the possible risk of humiliation and the possible threat to his upward mobility. But what he did not know was that Claude Bennet had left the day before to pursue a career in law at a boarding school in Pietermaritzburg.

At break of dawn there were several people outside Bennet's cottage; bearded men dressed in khaki outfits, sporting holstered revolvers, spoke in hushed tones. Curious natives and Indians stood at a respectful distance from the cottage. The air hung thick with gloom. Four young, khaki clad police constables carried Claudia Bennet's corpse on a stretcher to a waiting carriage. A sergeant questioned some men and noted information at intervals in a little notebook.

The sound of a galloping horse attracted everybody's attention; Bennet, looking visibly confused brought the horse to a standstill—slid down from the saddle and rushed to the carriage bearing his wife's body. Clearly, Bennet contemplated and measured his every act. He covered his face with his hands in despair.

"Who has done this?" he bellowed. A tall, burly, bearded farmer walked up to him and placed a sympathetic hand on his shoulder in an effort to console him.

"My beautiful Claudia!" he wept. The sergeant approached him respectfully.

"It must be a *coolie* or a *kaffir!*" he declared angrily.

"Sergeant!" he called out, almost incoherently, amidst tears.

"Find the man who did this!' The sergeant merely nodded his head and continued scribbling in his notebook.

Mathuray was a dark skinned indentured labourer. His cheeks were sunken in, giving prominence to his protruding facial bones. His glossy black hair was tied into a ponytail and his long aquiline nose did little to soften his features. His darting, quick movements resembled those of a ferret. His thin lanky frame fitted into an oversized shirt and pants. His shirt hung loosely over his pants, which was held up by a length of string tied around his waist; he wore no sandals or shoes. His feet were cracked and encrusted by a thick natural sole, developed over time through constant walking around barefooted.

Mathuray was employed by the Bennets to tend their garden. He loved his job—because it was far less strenuous than working in the cane fields and also because he felt special. The Bennets, on the other hand, had employed him because he appeared to be the most subservient of all the labourers; Mathuray was the most suitable to do their bidding.

John Bennet had already convinced the sergeant that the perpetrator must be a 'coolie'. Bennet had figured that Mathuray did not have the mental capacity to defend himself. To trump up a motive would not be difficult and given the fact that Mathuray had ample opportunity to murder his wife, he was an ideal suspect. Mathuray lived in the same barracks as Chandra. John Bennet had little problem in lighting the fires of gossip. Within a short while the little community was abuzz with the story that Mathuray had killed the *Sahib's* wife. As for the motive, the stories varied from theft to an inexplicable madness, which had possessed him. Some even ventured to add that Mathuray was so smitten by Claudia Bennet's beauty that he had become psychotically delusional and in a state of insanity had attempted to force himself upon her and had killed her in a fit of rage.

It was little surprise to the barracks community when Mathuray was led away by a sergeant and two constables two days after the murder. The three policemen, white men in uniform, towered above him when he answered the rapping on the door.

"You are Mathuray?" enquired the sergeant, in a very British accent. Mathuray nodded his head in acquiescence. The sergeant held Mathuray by the shoulder, twirled him around with relative ease and cuffed his hands.

"You are being charged with the murder of Mrs Bennet", he said, as he led him away to the waiting carriage. Mathuray did not have the faintest idea as to what was happening. He tried to register a protest in vernacular but he was ignored.

He found himself in a cell. The walls of the cell were crudely constructed with brick and mortar and a column of metal bars on one side leading into a long passage. Though spacious, the cell was cold, dark and dingy. A corner of the cell had a bucket filled with excrement of the inmates. Little lumps of excrement also spotted one corner of the cell. There were two others with him; they were natives. He held the bars of the cell and gazed vacantly into the passage, which led to the cell. One of the inmates urinated on the wall; the yellowish green fluid wound its way towards Mathuray and pooled around his encrusted feet—but he was completely oblivious of his surroundings. Large, purplish blue flies buzzed incessantly around the bucket of excrement and sometimes settled on the inmates. The putrid stench of faeces and urine permeated the whole cell.

When Chandra heard of Mathuray's arrest the following day, he was smitten with a deep sense of guilt. He knew that John Bennet was implicated in his wife's death; but to reveal what he had seen would compromise his position and jeopardise any hope that he may have of becoming a *sirdar*. The world was harsh and life had treated him poorly thus far. Away from the people whom he loved and cherished, away from a land that respected his pride and dignity—he felt alone and vulnerable. But he must survive! He must be strong so that he could go back to India to his people. In a strange and twisted kind of way he felt at ease with himself. But he felt an inner compulsion to visit Mathuray; whether it was to placate his own conscience or whether it was an obligation towards his fellow compatriot we will never know.

The following day, being a Saturday, all labourers were off duty. Chandra resolved to visit Mathuray at the holding cell in the village which was a good ten kilometres away. This would take him over two hours on foot. But there was a deep compulsion within him to visit Mathuray. He took leave of Baigum, who offered him the usual cup of tea, and he left while the sun was still ascending in the eastern horizon. The journey was long and arduous. After an hour he found that his sandals encumbered his progress. He removed them and walked barefoot the rest of the way.

Constable Barney was asleep at his desk and Chandra had to feign a cough to get his attention. The constable awoke with a shock, momentarily disorientated before he regained his composure. He led Chandra along a dark passage which led to a barred enclosure. Mathuray was asleep on the floor in a foetal position, covered with a thin grey blanket. Another two prisoners, natives, were seated on the floor with their backs against the wall. Without realising it Chandra found himself cupping his nose and mouth; he found the stench of faeces and urine overwhelming. The constable rattled the bars with his baton to awaken Mathuray, who awoke with a start, and on noticing Chandra, pushed the blanket aside and tottered sleepily, rubbing his eyes, towards him. Mathuray was happy to see him and for a moment he thought that Chandra was there to negotiate his release, only to be told that he was there out of concern. They spoke in Tamil in hushed tones although no one else could understand the language.

"Can you not speak to the Sahib? Tell him I didn't do anything!" pleaded Mathuray.

"I will talk to him." replied Chandra, guiltily, knowing full well that, that he had no intention of doing so.

"I cannot take this place anymore! We gave up our freedom in Bharat thinking that this was a land of promise? I must go back! Back to Bharat! Even if I have to live in abject poverty I will be a free soul! I did not come to this land to live in subjugation and slavery!" His eyes were glassy with tears. Pangs of guilt pierced Chandra with every word that Mathuray uttered.

"I believe in your innocence! I am sure the magistrate will have you released soon!"

But Chandra knew that the legal system was intrinsically biased against them and that the application and implementation of the law lacked consistency; the white man's law for the white man held greater sway than for the Indian or the African.

"*I would rather be dead than live another day within the confines of these walls; maybe I would be able to accept such punishment if I was guilty of an offence. But I am innocent!*"

"*Believe in God! He will take care of things!*" Chandra rejoined in his effort to console him.

"*All my life I dedicated myself to God. Yet I have known no happiness nor peace. I left Bharat but I never left God. I have engaged in prayer, meditation and constant contemplation of the divine, to the point where many have thought of me as being eccentric and a little insane. Where is this God? Where is this God that deems it fit to reward such dedication with this kind of life?*" Mathuray's lips quivered with emotion.

"*We do not know nor understand the ways of God. He has his reasons.*" Chandra said this to serve as an antidote to what he perceived as blasphemy.

"*This is a very cruel God Chandra. I always thought that God sows harmony, peace and eternal bliss. But I have seen discord, I have felt fear and anxiety, and I am not foreign to misery all my life. You too have had a fair share of sadness. We are God-fearing people. Is this our lot in life? God has forsaken me at a time I need him the most!*" Chandra was, for a moment, at a loss for words and even taken aback at Mathuray's eloquence and depth, nor could he find an appropriate comment to dissuade Mathuray from thinking such thoughts which he construed as blasphemy.

They heard the constable shout out from the end of the passage, "Time's up!" Chandra felt relieved; the interaction with Mathuray was becoming uncomfortably intense.

"*Do not worry! I will talk to the sahib!*" he said as he prepared to take leave of Mathuray. This time he was sincere about attempting to talk to John Bennet to coerce him into using his influence to have Mathuray released.

When the khaki clad Constable Barney made his routine rounds of the cells in the morning, little did he expect to be greeted by the sight that confronted him. He looked agape, his heart pounding uncontrollably and for a moment he stood transfixed. Mathuray's body hung lifelessly at the end of what appeared to be his shirt. His head was flopped forward and slightly angled; his tongue stuck out limply through the side of his mouth. The strong stench of ammonia was unmistakable from the dark patch of urine that had stained his pants around the crotch.

Constable Barney continued to gape, wide eyed and stricken with fear. He stood frozen for a good few seconds before he regained his composure.

"Sergeant!" he yelled while he simultaneously spun around to seek out his sergeant to handle a situation, which was clearly beyond the constable's coping mechanism. Sergeant Greene was already bounding up the narrow passage when he almost bumped into his Constable who was, by now, blubbering unintelligibly.

"Speak up, man!" demanded the Sergeant irritably. But the Constable lapsed into an uncontrollable bout of stammering. The Sergeant thrust the constable aside roughly and strode down the semi-dark passage towards the cell. It took a few seconds for his eyes to accommodate the darkness when he noticed the body hanging from the low rafter. The Sergeant was not moved by the tragedy that confronted him. He was repulsed by the thought of handling the body of a coolie. The acrid stench of ammonia together with the nauseating stink of human faeces which permeated the air, only served to agitate the Sergeant even more. Constable Barney was behind him, breathing heavily. He could almost feel the Constable's hot breath on the nape of his neck.

"Constable!" boomed the sergeant. "Go in there and release the coolie!"

The Constable was about to protest when the sergeant said, "Wait! That won't be necessary!" His gaze focussed on the two black prisoners who were cowering in the furthest corner of the cell. He gesticulated to them to approach him but there was no sign of any effort that that they we going to obey. Visibly agitated, and cupping his left hand over his mouth and nose, he bellowed at the natives to obey.

"Step up here, you silly kaffirs!" But the intended authority in the command was reduced to a muffled incoherent string of sounds as a result of his hand over his mouth. The natives would not have understood him anyway. They were still cowering at the corner of the cell when he drew his revolver and fired in the general direction of the natives. The explosive sound of the gunfire was amplified by the enclosed space. The bullet ricocheted off the walls and pinged with a sustained reverberation. The prisoners covered their ears instinctively with both their hands and reluctantly rose from their crouched positions. They gibbered unintelligibly and bent forward slightly in a subservient bow with their hands above their heads, without making direct eye contact with the sergeant. The Sergeant was somewhat relieved that the natives obeyed, especially since Constable Barney, a junior, was present. Sergeant Greene pointed to the lifeless body of Mathuray and with a combination of broken Zulu, English and gesticulations was able to communicate that they were required to release the noose around Mathuray's neck and to remove the body out of the cell.

Wide eyed with fear, one of the inmates clambered onto the shoulder of the other to get access to the knot; he worked frantically and the body slid down from the loosened knot and landed with a soft thud on the urine and faeces infested stone floor. One of the natives then held the corpse by the ankles and unceremoniously dragged it down the passage leaving streaks of mess in its wake.

The following day the barracks community was abuzz with the news that Mathuray had committed suicide. Speculations and gossip were rife. Women gossiped incessantly while doing the day's washing at the river. Men engaged in idle chatter while harvesting cane on the fields. Men and women never failed to put forth their theories and opinions, even at the communal toilets, where they were forced to meet.

The toilets constituted a row of holes in a crude wooden structure designed to accommodate the eastern way of squatting while defecating. The Indians were quite comfortable using the facility and there were times when a whole row of men would be simultaneously voiding their bowels while engaging in an idle banter, very often in Tamil, Telegu or Hindi.

All the gossip and speculations did little to assuage Chandra's deep-rooted feelings of intense guilt and regret. He was the only soul who knew the truth; he did not disclose this to even his closest friend and confidant, Baigum. Often, he would break out into a sweat at night when he had vivid dreams of Mathuray, glaring with blood shot eyes and pointing a gnarled and knotted finger accusingly at him. It was during these times that he valued the company of Baigum, who was always at his side. Although the relationship with Baigum had not graduated to the point of close intimacy, he was not unaware of Baigum's intense feelings for him. Yet, he could not bring himself to take Baigum as his wife — the memories of Shubnum frolicking and cavorting with him in the valley, away from the village, had never diminished even though time had passed. But Baigum never lost faith that someday Chandra would be her common – law husband.

Baigum, like most indentured labourers was alone. She had left her family in which she was the third born of eleven siblings to seek a better life in Natal. Life was difficult in India; there were many times when she pretended to have no desire to eat merely to ensure that the meagre meals would stretch enough to sustain the others. At twenty-four, she had often attracted the amorous attention of men, both young and old, but she would artfully deflect their advances and solicitations. When the recruiter had approached her one day, she was on the verge of warding him off when he mentioned recruitment for Natal and the immense wealth in Africa. The seed was sown. She knew, however, that her parents would never allow her to undertake such a venture to a foreign land. Despite the growing poverty they were closely knit as a family and the problem was compounded by the fact that she was a female in a male dominated society; females were perceived as being weak and entirely dependent on males. She reasoned that if she signed on secretly for emigration to Natal, the family would have one less mouth to feed. She would then be able to accumulate enough wealth to sustain her whole family when she returned.

The desire to leave the shores of India for Natal was nurtured and strengthened with every passing day, until she became steadfast in her decision and resolved to sign the relevant documents to be recruited. On the day of her departure, no one noticed the change in her demeanour and her attire when she left to visit the market in the local village. She stopped to turn around to look at her mother, who was sweeping the yard with the branches of a syringa tree. She stood, silently staring, and her eyes brimmed with tears.

It took only three months for Shiraz to become a whisper of his former self. His once proud girth withered away and his haughty and almost arrogant strides diminished into a subservient shuffling gait. He now walked with a hunch. His once sturdy, upright frame had disappeared.

Immediately after the whipping, Croft ensured that Shiraz was nursed back to health but he had never really recovered completely. To continue his torture, Croft employed Shiraz to tend to his horses. Psychologically it was a brilliant move. The whipping was a physical torture. Now Croft planned to persecute him emotionally and mentally. Croft was always there—a stark reminder of that dreadful day when Shiraz felt that he was being filleted alive. All this fed positively into Croft's psychological health. Croft was being more than adequately compensated for the humiliation he was subjected to in the shed. Now when Shiraz encountered Croft, he did not fail to assume a position of a reverential bow. Croft, on the other hand, was extremely pleased with his handiwork. He had systematically broken the spirit of this once proud individual. Day by day, week-by-week and month-by-month he had persisted in subjecting him to a planned and perfectly executed abuse. In fact, the whipping that Shiraz had endured had faded into insignificance against the mental torture to which he was now exposed.

Although, the task of tending to the horses was far less strenuous than working on the cane field, the thought of being near Croft all the time was a source of great anxiety and torment for Shiraz and Croft never failed to humiliate him in the worst possible way. For several days after Shiraz was employed as a stable hand, he was forced to eat horse dung while staring into the muzzle of a double-barrelled shotgun. The clods of digested grass being forced into his mouth made him retch but he had to swallow his vomit every time the muzzle of the rifle was thrust painfully against his forehead.

Shiraz grew weaker by the day. His only daily meal was the broth that was fed to him and the mongrel, which accompanied Croft on his hunting expeditions. He frequently broke into a sweat and grew tired easily and constantly complained of difficulty in breathing. On this day he felt particularly weak and chose to sit on a bale of hay in the stable. Croft walked in. Shiraz continued to sit which was contrary to his usual demeanour and this enraged Croft. As far as Croft was concerned, Shiraz was completely subjugated and this apparent show of defiance was a serious threat to his own sense of domination. Croft's anger was founded on acute fear for he had never recovered completely from the humiliation he had suffered at the hands of Shiraz.

"Get up, Coolie and get on your knees!" he barked. But Shiraz could not respond as quickly as expected by Croft. Croft strode up to him, and attempted to pick him up by the scruff of his neck. His task was made easier when Shiraz tried to obey by trying to stand. Croft sensed his weakness and seized the opportunity; he hurled himself against Shiraz, who went sprawling onto the dung-strewn floor. Shiraz lay face down — too weak to move. There was a brief moment of silence and then Shiraz felt a strange feeling of warm liquid trickling down his back. He turned, slowly and painfully, to establish the source of his discomfort while being acutely aware of Croft's presence. Croft was standing astride him and urinating while he smiled. In a flash his mind harked back to the dignity and pride of his tribe; he could almost see his ancestors astride galloping horses, brandishing flashing scimitars and charging into battle and his rage knew no bounds. At arm's length away, the nebulous form of a silvery grey metal spike took shape through his tear — filled eyes. Despite his weakness, the intense rage that he felt, appeared to have infused him with a new-found strength and determination. He reached out for the spike with his right hand while simultaneously using his left to hold onto Croft's booted leg to give him the necessary purchase to turn around to face Croft. Croft did not expect this. Shiraz lunged forward, spike in hand. As the spike penetrated Croft's thigh, the grating of metal against the femur was unmistakeable. With a howl of pain, he leapt back, shocked and enraged. It took him a few seconds to regain his composure. He drew his revolver and fired at point blank range at Shiraz's chest in quick succession. The sudden explosion of gunfire in the enclosed space was deafening. The horses whinnied and bucked.

Croft stumbled out of the stable. He squinted uncomfortably in the sunlight, having emerged from the darkness. The pain in his left leg was excruciating. He dragged it along limply while still holding onto the smoking revolver. Curious native servants rushed out. They looked but did and said nothing. Croft was acutely conscious of the sickly warm spurts of the arterial blood as it coagulated, sticking the cloth of his breeches to his skin. He was perspiring profusely. He had to make it to his cottage. But he could feel the clawing sense of nausea overtaking him—and then there was darkness.

When Doctor Smith rapped on his door the following morning, Croft was comfortably propped against snowy white pillows. Dr David Smith was a portly gentleman with an air of erudition about him that emanated from the notion that medicine was the preserve of an exclusive class of men. His chubby face sported a bushy brown moustache, which was painstakingly twirled at the ends. This, together with his thick-rimmed glasses gave him a benign, avuncular look. The silver chain that held his timepiece was conspicuous against his immaculate three-piece grey suite. 'Welcome back, Harold. We thought we had lost you', said Doctor Smith as he strode across to shake Croft's extended arm.

"You have been in a coma for the last twenty four hours and have lost a fair amount of blood". Croft looked confused and puzzled. "Twenty-four hours? All I remember is that ingrate of a coolie attacking me in the stable".

"Well that coolie will not be a threat to anyone anymore. You have done a good job of that!", exclaimed Smith.

"Why—what are you referring to?" Croft remembered every detail of the incident in the stable but feigned a lapse of memory.

"Don't you remember emptying your revolver into the Indian when he attacked you?" enquired Smith, with raised brows that creased his forehead into deep grooves as he pulled up a wooden chair.

"No! The only thing I remember is being attacked!" retorted Croft as he reached across for his pipe.

"You remember absolutely nothing?" asked Dr Smith probingly. Croft was silent as he sucked at his pipe causing hollows in his cheeks to accommodate the effort and the tobacco glowed healthily, filling the room with the masculine smell of rich tobacco.

"As I was saying", said Croft, between puffs of smoke, "I only remember being attacked".

Croft's agitation and discomfort did not go undetected.

"Harold! You should really stop smoking during this period of recuperation", said Dr Smith tactfully.

"You are also a diabetic and you have a pretty nasty wound on your thigh. It's not going to heal easily if you continue to smoke the way you do."

"You worry too much, David," interjected Croft, "I'll be fine! Anyway, smoking has nothing to do with anything!" replied Croft.

"I really don't know, Harold. There has been some talk that heavy smoking can aggravate a diabetic condition." responded Dr Smith.

"It's just talk! David! As I said, I'll be fine! You worry too much!"

But he was mistaken—how was he to know that he would be far from fine in the weeks and the months ahead?

⋯⋯⋯⋯⋯⋯⋯◆◇◆⋯⋯⋯⋯⋯⋯

With Chandra it was not only the memory of Shubnum that faded into oblivion like a passing cloud disappearing into the horizon; the memory of Claudia Bennet's murder and the false arrest and demise of Mathuray slipped, with each passing month into the remote and murky depths of denial and obscurity. Even India and all those he once loved and adored, faded into a diaphanous dream and Baigum had little problem in capturing his interest, with her artful coquetry. It was not long before she made the momentous announcement that she was pregnant. Chandra's delight was spontaneous. He flashed a smile that revealed a set of pearly white teeth through his bushy, black moustache. He circled his arm around her affectionately while he smoothed her hair tenderly with the other. From that day onwards he would always place his ear next to Baigum's abdomen to listen to any sign of activity within and when he felt the foetus kick, producing an unnatural lump in the taut skin, he would break into a smile, like a little boy who has just got his toy working.

Chandra and Baigum continued to work for Bennet. Their routine involved getting up before the break of dawn. Baigum usually used sticks and wood she had collected the day before to start a fire in the fireplace. Before long the coals would be glowing healthily and Chandra loved to gulp down the tea made from fresh cow's milk. The tea had a distinctive taste and smell but he relished it.

Then the two would set out with billycans of porridge, along the narrow footpaths towards the fields. There, they would toil continuously for several hours until they heard the sound of the whistle signalling a break for lunch.

Several times, Bennet had ridden up to the labourers, brandishing a whip and often he would even strike at a non-suspecting worker for stealing a moment to wipe his sweating face with the end of his caftan. On one of these occasions his son Claude had accompanied him, on horseback.

Like his father, Claude wore khaki pants with a matching khaki shirt. His hair was a bush of soft golden curls. At twenty-two years of age, he sported a fledgling growth of fine facial hair that added some degree of masculinity to his otherwise boyish look. His large emerald coloured eyes had a conspicuous softness, which contributed to his almost surreal allure. The dappled grey mare that he straddled bobbed its head in mild agitation as he tightened his reins to keep it still.

The large chestnut coloured stallion that Bennet rode stepped nimbly over clods of earth while Bennet allowed himself to bend and tilt in rhythm with the stallion's movement across the undulating ground. He held a half-plaited handle with coils of a leather strap of a whip in his right hand.

Siva, one of the labourers emerged from the thickets of a sugar cane plantation that was not being cut at that time. The cane parted, and he poked his head out gingerly in an attempt to join the rest of the workers without being noticed. But it was too late; Bennet caught sight of him as he tried to withdraw into the shadowy comfort of the plantation to escape from Bennet's wrath. Bennet was furious. He tugged at the reins and swung the steed around while simultaneously uncurling the strap of the leather whip. He was within whipping range in a few bounds. Siva, like most of the Indian labourers, was emaciated. He tried to run but only succeeded in hobbling on his spindly legs. Bennet leaned forward and struck. The thin leather strap curled around Siva's thin legs almost as if it had a life of its own. With a deft tug, Siva was brought down and he lay sprawled amongst the dry cane leaves and moist earth.

Bennet slid down from his horse when he heard his son call out, "Pa!"

He saw his son galloping towards him, "Don't do it, Pa!"

Bennet was on the verge of unleashing a well-placed boot onto the man's ribs when he froze on hearing his son's voice.

Confused and agitated, his face was puckered and creased, as he turned to face his son who had already slid down from the saddle, while the horse was brought to a slow canter. He walked up to the man, bent down on one knee, cupped the man's head with his left hand and propped him up into the sitting position.

Despite the obvious threat from Bennet, the labourers stopped working; they were clearly enchanted by the boy's presence and his act of kindness. By this time Bennet had regained his composure. "That's a coolie, son. They are heathens. You should not be touching them. Get away from him!"

This had no effect on Claude who stood up and extended his arm to help the man up.

"He must have left to pee, Pa. I don't think he deserves to be beaten for that!"

Bennet sensed the defiance and withdrew. He had no intention of engaging his son in an argument in the presence of the labourers.

As Bennet mounted his horse, someone hawked and spat. There was no mistaking Bennet's fury. He growled.

But on that day Claude had found a place in the heart of every Indian who was a witness on the field.

When the last traces of the rim of the sun had disappeared over the western horizon, Bennet lit the paraffin lamp on the rough wooden table. His mood had not improved. He pulled a wooden chair and slumped into it. With his elbows on the table propping his head he stared steadfastly at the yellow flame. For a moment he wondered at the stillness of the flame encased by the glass, shaped so much like a curvaceous figure of a woman — like Claudia. It had been almost six months since that fateful day when he had discovered a note underneath the vanity case which he had accidently tipped onto the floor. The note simply read, "Meet me tonight at the usual place".

This compounded the intense feeling of insecurity he had experienced in his marriage and exacerbated his very fragile relationship with Claudia. His mind harked back to the times when she shrugged away from his tender touch; it pierced him like a double-edged sword. But the note that he had found explained it all—the coldness and the contempt. He had to know with whom she had planned the rendezvous. "I will not approach her," He thought, "because that will alert her. I shall wait and keep a close watch on her. With time I will know."

They stopped sharing the bed. In fact, he had moved into the spare room over six months ago. She wanted it that way. Their relationship had been steadily deteriorating over the years but they lived together for Claude's sake. On the morning of that fateful day he heard Claudia's soft steps on the wooden floor. He crept out of bed, and as was his habit, he hurriedly strapped on his holster with the revolver and opened the door stealthily. He still had his khaki uniform on from the previous day. He had consumed a fair amount of whisky the night before and was too drunk to have changed into his nightwear. His head pounded incessantly and the stale taste of spent liquor raised his bile and he almost retched. He realised that his level of inebriation had not subsided completely as he held on to the furniture to ensure that he stepped firmly lest he stumbled. The thought of his wife plying her favours upon another male gnawed at him and worried him immensely. He felt the citric taste of acid well up in his mouth and he did not notice the low stool that Tembi, the maid had abandoned in the passage, after she had used it to reach the upper ends of the curtains that she had been dusting. He stumbled and then tried valiantly to break his fall by holding onto the drapes. But he only succeeded in bringing the entire curtain, with its rails, crashing down. He found himself sprawled in an undignified heap under the curtains. When he managed to clear the folds of the material from his face, he saw Claudia with folded arms, standing above him. She smiled, but the look of scorn, cynicism and contempt was unmistakeable. He tried to get up but his head was in a spin and he only managed to fall back on his buttocks.

Her words still rang in his ears. When she made a pointed reference to his manhood he felt his rage, which he had up to now managed to keep contained, erupt like an angry volcano. He did not see Claudia, his wife; he did not see the mother of his son; he only saw the object of his misery and woes. He stumbled after her into her bedroom. "Get out!" she rasped, as she swung around to face him. She caught a fleeting glimpse of the raging fire in his blood shot eyes as the open palm of his hand connected in a full-blooded impact against her face. She screamed once and then fell onto the bed without another whimper. The calloused, rough fingers of his right hand encircled her pale fragile neck. He felt the hardness of her larynx beneath the softish, tender skin and using his forefinger and thumb as a pincer, he pressed until he felt the tension in the cartilage of the larynx collapse.

That was six months ago but the memories were vivid and the scene was as graphic as if it had happened the day before. He reached out for the bottle of brandy that stood half full on the table and poured a generous helping into the glass. He raised it to his lips, threw back his head and emptied the contents in a few large gulps. Somehow he felt insulated from the world as the liquor burned its way through his gut and the recharged glass felt warm and comfortable within his grasp.

———

The first signs of winter receding were evident in the healthy green shoots making their appearance amongst the plants and trees, ravaged by the particularly harsh winter. Little sprigs of greenery peeked gingerly from carpets of grass that lay dormant and dry. The cane, too, assumed a conspicuous dark shade of green and whenever there was a breeze, ripples of waves undulated the tops of the cane amidst soft susurration of the long fronds as it whispered in rhythm with the breeze. Armies of finches and weavers pecked and bobbed as they hung inverted on the tree branches, in their effort to weave their nests of grass and leaves. It was at this time that Baigum lay supine on the grass bed of the barracks, in Chandra's crude apartment, in the clutches of acute labour pains. Two hours later, a baby girl was born.

Chandra was elated. Yet it was a strange kind of feeling; it was the first time he was completely responsible for another individual. And as the days rolled on, he did not consciously realise it, but his whole life pivoted around his family — Baigum and his daughter. Even his general demeanour and attitude was undergoing a gradual but definite change. His once altruistic attitude towards his fellow indentured labourers was being slowly eroded to be replaced by increasing acts of self-centredness. Whether this could be attributed to a sense of survival in a strange land or the fact that he was now responsible for the welfare of his family, one will never know. But several events thereafter made his fellow labourers wary of him — the kindness and sensitivity towards other labourers, which was characteristic of him, seemed to have evaporated.

Every indentured labourer was entitled to a weekly ration of a packet of mealie meal, mealie rice, sugar beans, dholl, sugar, rice and a bottle of oil. This was handed out on the Thursday of every week.

Siva was the community jester; nobody took him seriously. His moonlike, unshaven face displayed diversified shades of grey stubs. A fringe of grey hair encircled his bald pate and his incisors always protruded like that of a rodent. On this day he ambled in late and managed to secure a position in front to ensure that he was an early recipient of the ration. This transgression was always tolerated and relegated to his buffoonery and nobody paid much heed. Even when he boasted that he was able to swindle an extra bag of mealie rice they did not bother. In fact, some even chuckled in mild support. But on this day, Chandra, who normally kept aloof of such trivialities, strode up to Siva and verbally accosted him for his transgressions. Siva, in an attempt to slink out of a difficult situation, tried to dismiss Chandra with a cynical wave of his hand.

In an uncharacteristic move, Chandra lashed out with an open palm across Siva's face. A sudden hush descended upon the small crowd. Two men placed themselves strategically between Siva and Chandra lest the brief but unpleasant confrontation escalated to another level.

When all families had received their weekly ration, a lone figure made its way towards the Bennet's household. John Bennet was sitting on a wicker-basket chair sipping on a mug of coffee. On seeing Chandra, he immediately became alert and assumed a scowl, reserved only for the Indians.

"Yes! What is it that you want?" growled Bennet. "You should be on the field with the others!"

"*Sahib*, I got something very important to talk!" Chandra responded with some degree of trepidation.

"You? You, got something important for me?" queried Bennet curiously.

"Yes, *Sahib*! First matter is the coolies are stealing, sometimes, your ration. I caught one today." Bennet listened with a casual interest.

"So, why are you telling me this? What's in it for you?"

"*Sahib*, I can stop them! The only thing I ask is for you to make me your *sirdar*!"

Bennet had no intention of bargaining with a coolie. In fact, he was growing increasingly agitated.

"And what makes you think that I will make *you* the *sirdar*?"

"*Sahib*, I think you should make me your *sirdar*." Bennet thought that he heard the almost imperceptible trace of a veiled threat in his voice. But he shrugged it off. A coolie is never in a position to threaten. But the coolie's next statement sent a chill down his spine—it caught his attention. Suddenly, he felt debilitated; he could hear his heart pounding in his rib cage. But he had the presence of mind to know that he should desist from displaying his anxiety and fear overtly for it would elevate the coolie's bargaining strength.

"The night *memsahib* died — I saw master leaving the house in a great hurry. But I did not tell the police."

Bennet was quiet for a few moments; his mind was working in a frenzy.

"So you want me to employ you as the *sirdar*? I do not see a problem!"

Chandra was visibly happy with himself and his faint but conspicuous smile did not go unnoticed by Bennet. But he reasoned that not only would he be buying the coolie's silence but he would also ensure that he got the maximum out of the labourers.

Chandra sensed that he was playing the stronger hand in this agreement. He saw his opportunity and pushed.

"How much, master?"

"How much? How much, what?"

"I will now get the wages of a *sirdar*, master?" The change in title from *sahib* to *master* did not go undetected by Bennet.

Chandra agreed on two shillings more than that he earned as an ordinary labourer.

"One more small matter, master!"

Bennet was becoming increasingly agitated but he knew that this Indian was armed with information that was more deadly than a shotgun in his hands; this Indian not only stood between his freedom and imprisonment but also between himself and the love of his son, Claude.

"And what might that be?" pursued Bennet, trying valiantly to keep his rage under control.

"Master, if I have a horse, I will increase the cutting of the cane. The Indians will respect me more and I will control and oversee better!" Bennet reasoned that, *that* was a small price to pay for the Indian's silence. He nodded his head in silent agreement. Chandra walked back to his quarters in the barracks; he was happy with himself.

The community was abuzz with the news that Chandra was now a *sirdar*. As the days, weeks and months rolled on it was becoming increasingly clear that Chandra was no longer part of the common folk. He never stood in queues to collect his ration; he was no longer the recipient of juicy bits of gossip that were exchanged in lavatories and on the cane fields. Even his attire had undergone a drastic transformation. His traditional garb of dhoti and turban were replaced by a loose fitting pair of grey trousers, always with slightly oversize shirts. But the most significant transformation was his mode of transport; he no longer travelled on foot. He rode a chestnut brown mare; he was now aping the colonial whites.

Bennet no longer frequented the fields. It was Chandra who rode in at least an hour after work had commenced on the fields. Often he would sit in the shade against the bole of a large tree, sometimes carving apples, as he nibbled nonchalantly. But he always kept a watchful eye on the labourers and he never carried a whip, until one morning. He rode into the fields in the usual manner but this time he was clasping the plaited handle of a whip. He was conscious of the more than casual attention he was attracting but he pretended not to notice. He tethered his horse under the shade of a spreading mango tree and took his usual place from which point he commanded a good view of the labourers. The men watched him with antagonism before resuming their work. While working, they appeared to be engaged in some sort of robust discussion which alerted Chandra's curiosity. He strained his ears and without being too obtrusive, he ventured a bit closer. He was being discussed with great resentment over his sudden change in status. His reaction was more than a mild agitation. He strode up to the man nearest to him and confronted him with the coiled whip held firmly in his right hand.

"You have a big mouth!" he said in Hindi. The man barely picked his head up as he continued with the cutting of the cane. But he waved off Chandra with a slight flick of his left wrist— clearly a show of disdain and contempt. Chandra's fury knew no bounds. The whip was uncoiled, he stepped back in order to wield the whip effectively. The ensuing silence was sliced by the sudden crack of the whip. Its tapered end made contact with the man's back, ripping his shirt neatly; a second smart crack of the whip opened his skin revealing the white of his flesh. Little crimson beads pimpled the open wound. The man fell on his back trying vainly to protect himself from another assault from the whip by shielding his face with both his hands. But Chandra was done with the whip. His booted foot made contact with a dull thud against the man's side. The man bent double wincing with pain and coughing incessantly.

While most of the other labourers shouted profanities from a safe distance a few of the bolder ones were making their way towards Chandra to restrain him physically from any further assault on the man. Chandra sensed that the mood was growing ugly and considered it prudent to withdraw, while issuing a warning to the rest of the labourers.

Although Croft's injury had appeared to have healed he was never the same. A limp replaced his once authoritative gait and the slight but nagging pain was a source of constant discomfort. Worse, the fact that it was attributed to a wound inflicted by an Indian, who caused him great humiliation, and the fact that even in death he left behind an indelible scar and a permanent ache, raised his bile. He was acutely aware of the Pyrrhic victory he had earned by killing Shiraz. Although the matter was reported to the Protector and the Magistrate, Croft's action was attributed to self-defence and was never heard in court.

It was almost twelve months since the incident but the events were still graphically etched in his memory. He was also acutely aware that Dr Smith had constantly warned him of excessive smoking. And recently the constant pain goaded him to reach for the bottle more frequently. Dr Smith had cautioned him that although there was no conclusive evidence, there were indications that smoking could increase blood sugar levels and lead to insulin resistance. But Croft sought solace in the fact that this was not a proven fact and continued to enjoy his indulgence of tobacco.

Croft was seen less frequently by the Indians; his conspicuous lack of energy and enthusiasm to subjugate the Indians to his style of management and control was patently evident. Even his interest in his equestrian activities was greatly minimised. And the times he did mount his favourite steed, it was not without a measure of pain and discomfort. His sedate and fresh look, after horse riding, that was characteristic of him, was now replaced by a Croft that was out of breath and perspiring and a visage that was distorted by discomfort and pain. These days he had to be helped down from his horse. In February of 1863, Croft was not seen for the entire month. Speculations were rife that he had taken seriously ill and was confined to a hospital bed. He had appointed, Rathnam, an Indian of dubious reputation, as a *sirdar*, to oversee the labourers. Rathnam's appointment as a *sirdar* came as no surprise to the others. Everybody knew that Rathnam spied on his fellow workers; Croft was always in possession of information, which very often was a closely guarded secret. When he became the *sirdar* he continued to fawn openly in order to ensure that he maintained his position as *sirdar*. When the frequency of Croft's visit to the fields diminished, Rathnam walked taller than his five foot five. And he almost usurped the master's position. But his satisfaction of control and power was short lived.

The lazy silence of the midday was broken by the crunch of carriage wheels on the gravel surface, as a large carriage drawn by four horses, drew up in front of Croft's cottage. Steven Croft stepped out of the carriage. His shiny black boots, immaculate striped suit and conspicuous golden locks that peeked from under the rim of his bowler hat, set him apart from most other men of his race in that part of the world. His clean-shaven face and tall lean frame was actually a refreshing change from the usual khaki clad, bearded, dishevelled look of most of the employers. Steven Croft surveyed the landscape briefly as he panned the area with both his thumbs hooked into the pockets of his waistcoat. Amidst the curious stares of servants and labourers he walked up the path to the cottage while his suitcase was carried in.

Two hours later, Gogo, the house servant summoned Rathnam to report to the cottage. Rathnam was comfortably ensconced in a bed of hay in the shade of a spreading mango tree while he kept a watchful eye on the labourers as they harvested the cane. At intervals he would launch into a string of invectives in Hindi even if there were no real reason to do so. He believed that this kept the workers alert and deterred them from any possibility of slowing down. So, when he was summoned to the cottage to see Steven Croft, he was not only curious but nervous and anxious.

As he approached the cottage, he removed his old, large brimmed hat and held it respectfully against his chest as he stood on the veranda while tapping feebly on the door.

"Come in!" the loud masculine voice sounded hollow in the large cottage. Still clasping the hat with both his hands, he now assumed a slight, obsequious bow as he stepped in gingerly, after having removed his sandals at the door. The soles of his feet were dirty with mud from the field and they were thickly encrusted and cracked from constantly walking without shoes. His oversized pants rustled with every step he took.

He padded his way stealthily along the shiny wooden floor, pivoting his head nervously like a ferret. Steven Croft looked very relaxed and comfortable as he sunk himself in the soft cushion of the sofa. The corridor was so long that he appeared to be at the other end of a reversed telescopic lens. The tip of the cheroot glowed merrily as his cheeks hollowed while he sucked at his pipe with obvious pleasure. The arrogance and overt confidence of Rathnam's demeanour on the fields as a *sirdar* contrasted starkly with his timidity and obsequiousness as he approached Steven Croft.

"You understand English?" enquired Croft, authoritatively as he pouted his lips to let out a stream of smoke. Rathnam, continued to clasp his old, floppy wide brimmed hat deferentially, close to his chest as he nodded nervously.

"Well? Speak up man!" chided Croft, clearly agitated by Rathnam's apparent reticence.

When Rathnam responded with a "Yes *Sahib!*" his voice was barely audible. He repeated his response under the momentary threat of Croft's piercing glare.

"Well my brother, Harold, will not be able to return to the farm. He is not well. I am here to take care of some paper work."

Rathnam stood transfixed, twiddling his hat and looking vacantly at Croft.

"From tomorrow, you will no longer be working for the Croft family. You will be working for the Bennets."

Croft laid his glowing cheroot on the silver ashtray and reached out for the sheaf of documents before him. He pored over the documents while he gestured to Rathnam to leave, with a disinterested wave of his hand.

"Tell the rest of the coolies!" he remarked as Rathnam turned, with relief, to leave.

Rathnam scuttled out with the awkwardness of a crippled penguin. The bright sunlight made his eyes smart; he squinted till his eyes were slits in his dark face. He was troubled — very troubled. Although his comprehension of the English language was poor, he was able to gather that the farm would be changing hands. This had serious implications for him. He stood the very real threat of losing his position as *sirdar*. He was acutely aware of the fact that his fellow Indians disliked him. He could almost see the gloating visages, with cynical smiles of smug satisfaction, when the news of his impending demotion was revealed. It bothered him. He shuffled back to the field and resumed his place on the bed of hay but he was quiet — very quiet.

He was no longer interested in the usual gabble of the field workers, who continued to talk volubly, expecting the string of usual invectives to restrain them; but Rathnam just stared vacantly into the cane fields.

The relationship between John Bennet and Chandra, as the *sirdar* was never normal, in the context of the authority conferred upon the office of the *sirdar* and the accepted lines of communications between employers and *sirdars*. John Bennet rarely communicated with Chandra and he never acted forcefully or effectively in dealing with alleged misconduct by workers when reported to him. To John Bennet, having appointed Chandra as the *sirdar* was a matter of expediency and necessity. When the Croft farm was acquired John Bennet was only too glad to increase his workload by directing him to oversee both the farms without any added compensation. He also reasoned that he would be rid of him from his immediate vicinity. So, with the acquisition of the neighbouring farm belonging to the Croft family, he seized the opportunity of having Chandra transferred to the Croft farm. With the promise of a more spacious and comfortable living quarters, Chandra accepted the relocation with alacrity.

The following day, Chandra hitched the cart to the mare, his most prized possessions, loaded the few items of furniture and transported Baigum and his baby daughter to the cottage on the Croft Farm. Clearly, he had now attained a status, which was conspicuously superior to the other labourers — the cart, the horse and now a freestanding cottage. He was pleased with himself but he was also acutely aware of his vulnerability. He knew that he was disliked by his fellow labourers. He was not *unaware* of the fact that he had been ruthless in his aspirations. His upward mobility was primarily due to skulduggery. His aggression towards his Indian friends and acquaintances and the manner in which he was able to secure his position as a *sirdar* made him realise that his position was as strong as gossamer in the morning grass.

When he made his appearance on the fields of Croft Farm, the labourers had already commenced the cutting of cane. Men and women, armed with sickles, were spread out in the field, methodically and systematically harvesting the cane, leaving a distinct boundary between the field of uncut cane and that which had already been harvested. Chandra sat astride his mare, on the peak of the hill that overlooked the field and panned the landscape. He knew that he had to stamp his authority solidly and early. He prodded the horse with his heel and it set off at a trot in the direction of the workers. They did not notice him until they heard the cloppity-clop of the hooves on the sun-hardened track. They suspended their actions in the midst of their work to take in the strange sight of an Indian, armed with a whip, in western attire and mounted on a horse. They were less perplexed by his sartorial anomaly than they were by his whip and mode of transport. He held the reins with his left hand while his body tilted and swayed to the rhythm of the horse on undulating ground. His right hand clasped the handle of a whip, the tapered end of which dragged intimidatingly along the uneven ground with clods of turned soil.

To Chandra, seeing Rathnam in his favourite place under the mango tree was a conspicuously odd picture in the general landscape of sweat and toil. He got the horse to amble up to Rathnam, who realised that his worst fear and nightmare was about to materialise. Rathnam continued to be seated while the mare drew up next to him. He could feel and hear the thumping of his heart in his rib cage. The horse appeared nervous and agitated as Chandra held the reins taut to maintain control. He leaned forward in his saddle and pointed the whip at Rathnam and addressed him in Hindi.

"You should be working like everybody else!"

"I am working!" replied Rathnam defiantly. *"I am the sirdar!"*

"This farm now belongs to the Bennets! You are no longer the sirdar! Now join the others on the field!" commanded Chandra.

Work on the field had come to a standstill. All attention was being focussed on the drama that was unfolding.

"Move! Or feel the bite of this whip!" Chandra hissed between clenched teeth. Chandra, too, could feel his heart pounding. He knew that all eyes were focussed on him; he had to stamp his authority now! Whether Rathnam continued to sit because he was too petrified to consciously effect any movement or whether he refused to obey as a show of defiance, one will never know. When Chandra cracked the whip, the tapered end curled itself around Rathnam's neck, like a serpent. Almost simultaneously, Chandra tugged while the horse whinnied and bucked. Rathnam found himself yanked bodily from the bole of the tree against which he was leaning. The action had also acted as a noose around his neck. His eyes bulged, almost popping out from its sockets. He kicked vainly in an attempt to obtain purchase with his feet but Chandra

had already slid down from his horse. He used his left booted foot to pin down Rathnam's flailing right arm while the outer edge of his right foot was placed firmly on Rathnam's neck at the point of his larynx, while still clutching the whip. Rathnam only managed to emit a guttural sound while he tried in vain to dislodge himself from under Chandra's weight.

"There can never be more than one sirdar! Remember that!" Chandra's voice was almost a whisper.

Rathnam lay on his grass bed in his room in the barracks. He stared vacantly at the crude wooden roof. The events of the day played itself over and over in his mind. The bruise around his neck was still raw and the pain in his larynx did little to ease the mental turmoil he was experiencing. Every time he slid into sleep, a hundred hands clawed at his throat and the faces of Steven Croft and Chandra morphed, moulded and transformed with ectoplasmic agility and he sat up troubled and perspiring. His intense hatred for Chandra burned and flared and his anger was a cauldron of seething rage. He had to do something! He had to do something to extricate himself from the mental anguish! He had to do something for his own survival and his psychological well-being.

He watered and nurtured his hatred and it grew bigger and stronger every hour. The following day he did not report to the field. In the seclusion and privacy of his dark, dank room, he planned and conceived. He saw himself armed with a wooden club and a sickle, crouching in the shadows of the moonlit night; he saw Chandra opening the door of his cottage to make his way to the latrine; he could almost hear the heavy club thudding against his skull and the crunch of bones. He saw Chandra crawling and grovelling at his feet, begging for mercy. And his eyes creased into slits and he smiled.

The air was cold and crisp and the night was dark. In times like these there were hardly any persons outside the barracks; everybody stayed huddled in bed or sat around a make-shift brazier, either indoors or outside. The brazier was usually a perforated twenty litre metal drum in which chunks of coal were lighted to serve as a heater. Rathnam left his quarters to scout the area to ensure that there was no activity outside. This did not take long. He returned to his quarters and placed the wooden club, which he had fashioned from the branch of a tree, into a sack. He stepped out into the night air and made his way with a single-minded resolve towards Chandra's cottage.

Chandra was never the loquacious type. His perennial reticence was accepted as being naturally characteristic. He was one of those persons who never believed in speaking about one's anxieties or stresses. But on this day even Baigum detected that Chandra was not his usual reticent self—he was morose.

"Is there something wrong, my husband?" she enquired with concern.

Chandra who had been sitting on the wooden chair, his elbows resting on the table, propping his face in deep contemplation, did not respond immediately. Slowly and deliberately, he turned to look at Baigum, who was engaged in stoking the fires to cook the evening meal.

"Yes! I'm troubled! Yesterday I beat up a man! I didn't want to but I had no choice!"

"But you had done that before. Why are you troubled now?" Baigum continued to stoke the fire.

And as destiny would have it, it was at this time that Rathnam had been crouching in the shadows, beside Chandra's cottage, waiting to execute his plans. He knew that it was around this time that Chandra would leave his cottage to visit the lavatory which was about fifty paces away from the cottage. But the voices from within the cottage galvanised his attention; his interest and curiosity piqued. He was oblivious to the low hum of the multitude of insects. The sound of the voices from within the cottage was crisp and clear in the silence of the night.

"I have lost the faith and the trust of the people. I wish I had earned the position of sirdar. Then I would have commanded respect. Now I have to demand respect and compliance!" said Chandra, while he continued to stare emptily at the fire.

"I don't understand!" Baigum suspended stoking the fires and looked up quizzically with creased brows.

"There is something I have never told you!" replied Chandra.

Rathnam pressed his ears closer to the wall. His heart was pounding and he was breathing heavily. For a moment he was afraid that he might be detected.

"I know who murdered memsahib!" Chandra leaned back against the chair and looked at Baigum—focussing attention on her for the first time during the conversation.

Rathnam's excitement was spiralling.

"You know who murdered Memsahib?" demanded Baigum with a tilt of her head and looking perplexed.

"Yes! And it was not Mathuray!" responded Chandra.

Rathnam did not realise it but despite the cold breeze, his forehead was pimpled with beads of perspiration. His breathing was uncontrollably deep and quick. It was imperative that he did not miss a single syllable or word that Chandra was communicating. He knew that the revelation would be a potent ammunition against the one individual whom he hated intensely.

"It was the Sahib, Bennet!"

Baigum covered her face partly using the edge of her sarie and stared at Chandra, imploring him silently to continue for she was confused and shocked at the revelation.

"Nobody else knows this. You are the first person I have ever mentioned this to."

She continued to listen silently as the full revelation of his acquisition of his position of *sirdar* unfolded. Her emotions traversed from anxious concern to stressful anxiety as she realised that her husband's position and the very livelihood of the family hinged on the confidentiality of this bit of information. She now became aware of the tenuous nature of Chandra's position as *sirdar.* But little did she realise that her whole world was about to crumble around her. Little did Chandra realise that he had unwittingly armed someone with a weapon more potent than anything he could imagine.

Rathnam walked back to his room in the barracks a good five hundred yards away. For the first time in many days he felt at ease and light-hearted. The sickle-shaped moon appeared to be almost smiling as the diaphanous edge of a dark cloud veiled it momentarily, creating an illusion of it sailing in the night sky.

The morning sun had already ascended and blazed intensely above the treetops. A slight breeze occasionally ruffled the leaves as Baigum cradled a large wicker basket of clothes to be washed at the stream. It had become almost a tradition for the women of the village to gather at the stream every Monday morning to wash the clothes in the flowing waters.

At this point the stream was characterised with a tumble of rounded brown and grey boulders of all sizes and shapes. Refracted images of cobbled stones and sandy substratum of the river flickered and danced to the rhythm of the rapidly flowing surface, as the stream gurgled and washed over the stones and boulders. The women of the village looked forward to this rendezvous. No less than a dozen of them would assume their regular positions at rocks and boulders to execute their tasks of washing the clothes. Soapsuds and foam would circle their bangled feet and then rush away as it got arrested with the flow and coalesced with the rest of the stream further down. During this time there was never a moment of silence as the women often engaged in idle chatter and village gossip. Baigum enjoyed these moments too. But on this day she was not her usual buoyant self. She was deep in thought, pondering over the information she had received from Chandra the night before. She could not, however, place a finger on the exact source of her anxiety. She was confused. She respected and loved her husband and yet there was a part of him she did not know. And that gave her cause for concern.

"*Why?*" she thought, "*why did he not reveal the truth when he ought to have done so? Why did he allow an innocent man to be imprisoned and subsequently lose his life? Why? Why?*"

She was almost completely oblivious to the multitude of cackling voices, sometimes in Hindi but often in Tamil or Telegu, until she heard:

"*Mathuray did not kill the sahib's wife!*"

It caught her attention. This was not common knowledge. While the rest of the women discussed, challenged and exchanged information spiritedly, yet without an element of seriousness, Baigum's face reflected deep concern and apprehension. The coincidence was too much. Just when she was in possession of purportedly confidential information, the whole village was in possession of this bit of intelligence. How? Her husband was bound to think that she had been responsible for having leaked the information. The implications were frighteningly detrimental to her personal welfare and yet she knew that she was as innocent as her baby that she had left in the care of the *ayah* next door. She raised her head slowly and deliberately, taking an interest for the first time in the spirited dissemination of what they perceived as a significantly juicy bit of entertainment.

"*Are you mad? Mathuray did kill the memsahib!*" interjected a portly grey-haired woman as she hefted a large item of her laundry, to beat upon the rock, to remove stubborn stains and dirt.

She was quite breathless as she continued, *"I really don't know where you people get such information!"*

"The whole village is talking about it!" replied a dark-skinned woman, sporting a large ring on her left nostril, cradling a naked baby on her hip, while standing on the bank.

"Then who killed the sahib's wife?" enquired Baigum, anxiously waiting for a response.

"The sahib!" piped Maliga, the village gossip.

While this sent a chill down Baigum's spine, the others broke into a gaggle of laughter to hear such ludicrousness. Her heart was pounding and her legs felt heavily weighted as she gathered the few items of clothes she had washed and made her way towards the bank. She released her sarie that was rucked above her knees and made her way home, carrying the wicker basket and burdened with anxiety.

Chandra entered the field, sitting astride his mare. With the whip held ostentatiously in his right hand and the reins with the left, he deliberately allowed the extended whip to drag menacingly along the ground. He was relieved to see Rathnam busy with rest of the labourers on the field. It was necessary for Chandra to entrench his authority solidly to ensure that there were no opposition to his position as a *sirdar* in the future. He rode up to where Rathnam was working and brought his mare to a standstill. Rathnam continued to cut the cane while he turned to look at Chandra who fixed his gaze upon him. But Chandra was uneasy; Rathnam had a cynically satisfied expression — incongruous with the events of the previous day.

Though disturbed, he retired to the shade of the mango tree, after having tethered his horse. Resting against the tree, he chewed unconsciously on a reed of grass, as he wondered about Baigum and his baby daughter. He felt happy and contented at the very thought of them. Baigum made a fine wife and she had given him a lovely daughter.

It was Thursday — the day on which families looked forward to collecting their rations. The usual indistinct queue stretched about twenty yards from the dispensing office. Chandra occupied a seat behind the desk with a sheaf of papers before him. Two aides handed out the rations under his direction. As the labourers filed past they were spiritedly and volubly engaged in the South Indian dialect of Tamil. He usually took no interest in what he considered to be idle and inane chatter but today was different.

"Mathuray died in vain!" exclaimed a slightly hunched very dark skinned Indian with a discoloured, once white dhoti and a turban to match. He continued with the characteristic click of the tongue to express pity and sympathy.

Chandra's interest was piqued.

"But is this really true?" enquired another sceptically.

Siva, whom Bennet had accosted on the cane fields, had a balding pate which, burnt by the sun, contrasted starkly with a white fringe of hair. He responded with alacrity, *"Everybody knows it must be true!"*

"What is true?" enquired the other.

"That Sahib Bennet killed memsahib!" responded Siva with smug satisfaction.

Chandra froze. His forehead became furrowed as his eyebrows tensed. His concentration wavered. The ration dispensation was momentarily suspended as Chandra lapsed into silence. The man, next in line, stood visibly bewildered. Chandra instructed one of his helpers to continue with the dispensing of the ration and he left hurriedly.

Chandra was a troubled man that day, as he rode home on his horse that cantered, without any prompting, along the usual route. There was still about an hour of sunlight as the sun bathed the western horizon with a pinkish red glow and the tall conifers formed distinct silhouetted outlines against the setting sun. His mood was sombre as he considered whether there were any other possibilities of how the information about Bennet's involvement in the murder could have leaked to the community. There was no other way it could have happened besides through Baigum. The coincidences were too much. He had discussed it with Baigum for the first time the night before and she was the only one to whom he had ever mentioned it—the next day the whole community knew about it. *"She definitely cannot deny it!"* he thought. The only thing he needed to know was how she did it and why. Scraggy dogs with mangy coats yelped and barked dutifully as he passed the community barracks; the horse trotted on nonchalantly.

He was still deeply engrossed in his thoughts as he approached his cottage. He tethered his horse and walked up the short pathway leading to his cottage. He could feel and hear the sugary gravel crunch under his booted feet—it's funny, he thought, he had never noticed it before.

Baigum was seated on the floor darning his trousers in the panel of light that made its way through the open shutter. She picked up her head briefly when Chandra entered. She was apprehensive. The child, just over a year old, on seeing her father, tottered unsteadily with extended arms towards him, entreating him to carry her. He scooped her up and cradled her in his usual manner. He sat on the crude wooden bench close to the fireplace, where a pot was steaming lazily as the lusty flames licked the sides. The child whom he had seated on his lap, wriggled impatiently to be put down so that she could return to her rag doll with which she had been playing. Baigum stuck the needle into the material she was sewing and made her way towards a large, slightly chipped enamel cup to prepare tea with fresh cow's milk. This was the daily routine when he returned from the fields. Usually they would engage in idle chatter. But today was different. As the seconds ticked by the silence was broken by Chandra.

"Did you know that the whole village knows the information that I had given you last night? I had spoken to nobody else!"

"Yes! I know!" replied Baigum apprehensively.

"Whom did you tell?" he asked, trying valiantly to control his rage.

"I told nobody!" she replied emphatically.

"You are lying!" he barked viciously.

"How else would anyone know? Is it a coincidence that I confess to you the night before and the following day the whole village is in possession of the information?"

Chandra was bristling with anger.

"When I heard it while washing at the river I too was upset and surprised! Believe me my husband! I will not do or say anything to hurt you!" she shot back.

"How else would anyone in the village know if it's not through you?" he glared viciously at her and stood up with clenched fists, desperately trying to bring his emotions under control. Baigum sensed his intense fury. She noticed the crazed madness in his eyes and cowered nervously near the fireplace, while tugging the ends of her sarie to cover her face as she sobbed. Then, impulsively, she stooped at his feet and encircled her arms around his legs, in an attempt at entreating him to believe her.

"Can you not see that an injury to you affects me and the baby?" she sobbed.

But his rage was all consuming. He held her by the shoulder and shook her off; he shoved her disdainfully with his foot. She lay sprawled on the floor while the child stared wide-eyed, still clutching the rag doll. Chandra made for the door, slid the barrel-bolt lock with a loud clatter and stepped out into the dusk.

The sun had set but the western horizon was splashed with an orange tinge and the tall conifers formed distinct silhouettes against the outline of the craggy peaks. A multitude of insects filled the night air with an orchestra of sounds as they hummed and creaked like a single organism. It had been a long time since he had thought of home — of his mother, his father, his brother and most of all Shubnum and the humble cottage in the deep South. He wished he was at home and his heart was heavy.

Ann Russell was happy. She felt a lightness of spirit as the chestnut brown stallion she was riding clip-clopped lazily over the cobbled stones of the dry riverbed. She was looking forward to her meeting with Claude Bennet. They had been meeting secretly for over a year now. Both Claude and Ann knew that their parents would not approve of their relationship because of the intense rivalry between the families. Furthermore, John Bennet's vile temper was no secret. It was unfortunate that Ann's parents had judged Claude to be like his father. But the politics and the animosity between the families did not bother them. They kept it out of their relationship. Ann was young and sprightly. At twenty-two years, she was full bodied and beautiful. Her golden curls flowed abundantly from beneath her bonnet. Her tweed shirt strained coyly against her firm petulant breasts. Her trousers, which hugged her provocatively appealing buttocks, were tucked into a pair of brown leather boots.

Claude was seated underneath a tree. His horse was tethered fifty paces away. Ann slid off her horse and slapped it gently on the rump. It cantered away to graze close to Claude's mare. The rays of the sun created a halo around her golden locks and Claude marvelled at her beauty. He circled his arms around her slender waist and kissed her hungrily.

They spoke very little as they hugged and kissed, compensating for the hours they were away from each other. Then, they chatted. It was almost a routine. But today's conversation was not the usual lighted hearted banter in which they normally engaged. With her head resting on his shoulders, while he leaned against the tree, she said, "Mary, the Coolie maid mentioned that all the villagers were saying that your father had something to do with your mother's murder!"

She tried to sound casual in order to dilute the sting of a patently incriminating statement. She felt his strong fingers dig into her as he pushed her away to hold her at arm's length.

"What did you just say?" he queried disbelievingly.

"It's probably nothing Claude! It's just village talk! The coolies are always looking for something to engage their idle tongues!"

But her attempt at rendering the circumstances innocuous and harmless was futile. Village talk it might very well be but flashes of his father physically abusing his mother and his constant state of drunkenness had lent credibility to it. The seed had been sown and already it was being watered and nurtured in fertile ground.

"I have to talk to Mary!" he uttered in a shocked voice. Without realising it, he held her at arm's length and shook her like a puppy agitating a rag doll.

"Claude! Stop it! You are hurting me!" she cried out. He snapped out of his daze and released her apologetically.

"I'm sorry! But I have to speak to Mary!"

"I shall try to get you to meet with her, but it will be difficult. Mary is constantly busy at home. She will be missed even if it is for a short while." Ann pushed him away gently, stepped back and surveyed him with folded arms.

"But I need you to help me, Ann! Please!" Claude insisted.

"Claude! This is village talk! Please let it be! It will blow over!" she implored dolefully.

"You don't understand, Ann! What if it's true? I have to know! I have to speak to her! Please!"

They bid farewell in the usual manner but Claude's mood was as dark as the clouds that hung over them and Ann rode off with a heart burdened with the impending threat of losing the comfort, thrill and excitement of the usual rendezvous.

Mary Gabriel was a devout Christian Catholic, petite with short black hair and slightly lighter skin than most of the field workers and conspicuously devoid of such adornments as nose studs and rings. She was always clad in white frilly dresses that hung just below her knees. A distinctive feature of Mary Gabriel was that she not only spoke English fairly competently but she had also embraced much of the culture of the whites to the extent that she frowned upon the Hindu field workers. She had been working for the Russell family for over a year and they had come to recognise that she was what they perceived as being less of a heathen than her fellow countrymen. She tried her utmost to imitate her employers in every way possible and she longed for her skin to be as light as theirs. The fact that they treated her as a being that was inferior to them in every way, was acceptable to her. On Sundays, she together with the rest of her family, attended church with the Russells. But they were relegated to an obscure, remote part of the church, away from the white congregation. The Solomons, another Indian family, joined them regularly on Sundays. Mary looked forward to the Sunday sermon, especially the after-church meeting with the Solomons. They usually met outside the church where they sat on a cushion of soft green grass. While both fathers engaged each other on the issues of labour—both were *sirdars* in their respective farms—the children played and the women caught up with the latest gossip, very often in their native tongue of Telegu. It was at one such meeting that Mary learned that the *sirdar* of Bennet's farm was a prime witness to Claudia Bennet's murder and the startling revelation that John Bennet was indeed the perpetrator of this horrible deed.

The source of this intelligence was Peter Solomon who took more than a casual interest in Mary. Peter Solomon was no more than twenty five years old. Like most Indian men, he was short by western standards, at five feet seven; he was clean shaven with jet black hair that was neatly plastered to his scalp. His face appeared gaunt as a result of his protruding cheek bone and his taut skin. He had the peculiar manner of pivoting his head in quick staccato movements, much like a rooster ferreting for food. He was particularly proud of his overly large fawn suit, which helped to cover his slight frame. Peter was only too enthusiastic to part with this bit of intelligence even if he was rewarded with just a fond touch from Mary. Given the fact that suitable, eligible bachelors were rare and searching for one of a Christian faith, narrowed the field even further, Mary too, was somewhat attracted to him. But they had very few opportunities of nurturing and growing this relationship which was very much in its embryonic stages. Peter Solomon looked forward to the Sundays and he would often plan how he would keep Mary interested for the time he was with her, however short it might be. But he was more than pleased with himself when he had engaged Mary with the afore mentioned information. What he had deemed to be just juicy village talk had Mary gripped in rapt attention for she knew that Ann would be very interested.

It was a Wednesday morning. On this day Mary's chores were decidedly minimal for most of the routine tasks would have been completed. Ann, therefore, had arranged for Claude to meet with Mary at their usual rendezvous. It was planned that Mary should feign illness and inform Clara Russell, Ann's mother, of dizzy spells that she was experiencing.

While Ann sat astride her horse which trotted lazily along the rutted path, Mary walked briskly alongside. The morning was bright and the sky was cloudless. Usually, Ann would look forward to the meeting but today was different. She was filled with apprehension. She noticed Claude from a kilometre away when the path curved bringing Claude into the line of sight. Even from a distance she noticed that he was not his usual, light-hearted self. He would normally be seated, resting against the usual tree, lazily chewing a reed of grass while waiting for Ann. But on this day Claude stood gazing along the road while holding on to the reins of his mare as it bobbed its head in mild agitation. Ann's anxiety impelled her to prod the horse into a canter leaving Mary behind to catch up. She slid off the horse to approach Claude and enjoy a brief moment of an affectionate embrace while Mary was still a good distance away.

"Hello Claude!" Ann's voice was almost a whisper.

"Hello Ann!" He responded perfunctorily. She curled her arms around him and snuggled her head in the crook of his neck but he did not reciprocate. She pulled away angrily.

"Is this how it's going to be every time you have a problem with the world, or is it me?" she hissed at him.

"It's not you Ann! Please understand!" he replied.

"God knows, I'm trying Claude!" she rejoined in an attempt to break through the armour he had built around him.

"Losing a mother, is bad enough, Ann! But to have her plucked away prematurely and the manner in which she died is hard to come to terms with."

"Believe me I know!" she rejoined. "You need me Claude! We need each other! Don't push me away!" she pleaded. They did not notice Mary who stood a respectful distance away waiting to be summoned. Mary attracted their attention with a delicate cough. "Claude, this is Mary, the coolie maid, I have been telling you about", said Ann introducing Mary who continued to stand twiddling her thumbs. Ann beckoned Mary to approach. Mary approached but continued to keep a respectful distance between them. Claude tethered his horse to an overhanging branch of a tree and walked towards Mary. He continued to stare at her. The maid looked uneasy and refused to look Claude in the eye.

"Tell me what you know!" he demanded. Both Ann and Mary sensed the intensity of his emotion and his determination in his quest for the truth. But Ann knew that given Mary's very fragile nature, Claude would not be successful in eliciting the desired information with the approach he had adopted.

"Let me handle this, Claude!" requested Ann, laying her hand gently on Claude's shoulder. Ann beckoned Mary to follow her as she made her way to a green patch of grass in the shade of a tree.

Mary felt at ease as she sat with her legs folded neatly beneath her while Ann found a rock on which she perched herself. Claude continued to stand with his arms folded.

"Now, don't be afraid, Mary!" said Ann comfortingly. "Tell us what you have heard."

Mary continued to twiddle her thumbs, with her head bowed.

"Come, Mary! Don't be afraid!" prompted Ann.

"The big boss killed *memsahib*!" blurted out Mary.

Claude furrowed his forehead as he raised his brows.

"I suppose you are referring to my father?" Claude probed to ensure that there was no misunderstanding.

"How do you know this?" demanded Claude grimly.

"My father told us!" responded Mary, "He heard the men in the field talking. They also said that the *sirdar*, Chandra, saw it happen."

The mention of Chandra piqued Claude's interest.

"Chandra? The fellow who works for my father?" he enquired looking perplexed and with lines of anxiety etched on his face. Mary nodded her head while looking at Claude for the first time.

"Are you absolutely sure, Mary?" Ann probed. Mary nodded again while looking at Ann.

"You may leave now Mary!' Ann ordered. 'Don't tell Mama that I am with Claude. I will be in shortly!'

Mary nodded her head in timid acknowledgement and directed her steps towards the farmhouse.

"What now Claude?" queried Ann.

"I am going to confront Pa!" he replied.

"Should you not question the worker first?" Ann asked with concern

"No! If I did that I somehow feel that I would be betraying Pa. I am sure there is no truth in it."

They mounted their horses and Claude galloped off. Ann watched him disappear in a cloud of dust while her horse fidgeted skittishly.

John Bennet was at the cow-pen reprimanding Temba, the cowherd, for some omission that Temba himself was not sure of. John Bennet's reputation as a dedicated farmer and competent farm manager had been whittled away over the years, more especially after the death of his wife Claudia. His constant state of inebriation, his slurred speech, his failure to attend to routine farm matters and his slovenly attire led to a general lack of diligence and commitment from the farm labourers. When he saw Claude come galloping towards the pen he was momentarily distracted from his attempt at censoring Temba.

"I need to talk to you, Pa!" Claude's voice had a sense of urgency.

"I am busy—will see you later!" retorted Bennet, despite the unmistakeable air of seriousness he detected.

"No! I want to see you now!" For a moment Bennet thought he detected a subtle but unmistakeable tone of disrespect. But his curiosity overwhelmed the agitation he felt at the perceived change in attitude.

"Very well! I shall see you *now*—if that's what you want!" Bennet stood scratching his head thoughtfully as he watched Claude gallop off towards the cottage.

Claude was seated at the wooden table. He looked uncharacteristically pensive and somewhat truculent with his chin propped up by his interlaced fingers. He continued to stare vacantly ahead of him as his father walked in. John Bennet noticed a conspicuous change in attitude and felt a sense of foreboding. He felt his pulse racing and his heart pounding.

"Sit!" ordered Claude. Bennet found himself obeying. He did not realise that this was a reversal of the normal order of roles. The chair scraped annoyingly on the wooden floor as he dragged it out and perched himself awkwardly at the edge of the seat.

"Well, here I am!" Bennet could feel the thumping in his rib cage.

"Tell me the truth!" Claude's voice was almost a whisper. Bennet froze. Had the day that he had been dreading all these months finally arrived? It took a few seconds for him to regain his composure. Perhaps there was still a hope that he could slip out of a situation that could spell his ruin.

"Truth? What truth?" enquired Bennet looking visibly perplexed.

"The *truth* about Ma!" responded Claude — raising his voice.

"Everything I know, *you* know! What *else* can I tell you?" demanded Bennet.

"There is talk amongst the coolies that . . . . that . . ." he could not bring himself to make a pointed reference to his father's involvement in his mother's murder.

"That you had something to do with Ma's death!" Claude blurted it out, almost as if he wanted to get over saying it.

Although Bennet had sensed all the time that Claude's belligerence was connected to Claudia's demise, he was still visibly ruffled when Claude made a pointed reference to his mother's murder.

"That's nonsense! You know as well as I do that it was that Indian coolie! Where is this coming from?" demanded Bennet.

"Your *sirdar!*" replied Claude grimly. He so longed to hear his father give him a reasonable explanation, so that the village talk could be relegated to gossip mongering and that they could continue with their lives, despite the void left by his mother's death.

Bennet felt a burning anger within him. He knew that if he did not take control now it would escalate into an uncontrollable rage. He still nurtured a hope of extricating himself. He dared not lose the one thing that had made his life worth living — the love of his son. The coolie had not kept his word. But why? Had Claude spoken to him? What did Claude know?

He has to be aggressively defensive and perhaps it would buy him enough time to speak to the coolie.

"So you choose to believe the gossip of those lowly coolies and take up cudgels against your father?" he bellowed.

"I don't want to *believe* them, Pa! I want to hear you say something — that . . . that you had nothing to do with this whole sordid business!" Claude's use of the term of endearment, "Pa" did not go unnoticed by Bennet. He found a chink in the armour and he exploited it.

"Yes! Your mother and I never saw eye to eye on all counts. But I would never harm a hair on her head. Did that coolie, Chandra feed you with this story?"

"I have not spoken to him yet, Pa!" replied Claude defensively.

Bennet breathed a sigh of relief. There was still a hope of manipulating the situation. He reasoned that the Indians were easily swayed with the offer of incentives and rewards.

"Then where did you get these ridiculous allegations from?" rejoined Bennet, who had by now recovered sufficiently from the initial shock of the impending threat of being exposed and was using his confidence to stay ahead of the game.

"From Ann's coolie maid, Mary." replied Claude. Despite his state of emotional upheaval and his intense anxiety, he felt instinctively that he should mention Ann as a way of breaking her into the barrier that existed between the families.

"Who is Ann?" queried Bennet curiously.

"The girl I have been seeing secretly for over a year now."

"Why the secrecy?" rejoined Bennet.

"Because, Pa, they hate you! And I know that you dislike them intensely. Remember the time you almost beat up Ma because she greeted Anna's father, Peter Russell?"

But Bennet was hardly listening. His mind harked back to the note he had found. Was it possible that the note had belonged to Claude. His mind was in a turmoil. He stared vacantly and lapsed into silence.

"Pa! Are you listening? Pa?" Claude thumped the wooden table in agitation with the side of his fist. This shook Bennet and brought him back from his momentary reverie.

"Yes . . . yes! I'm listening. I'm just disturbed that we are still reeling from the death of your mother and now we have these malicious rumours about me. It's all too much!"

"I will investigate further and get to the bottom of it, Pa!"

Whether he intended investigating to clear his father's name or to establish the truth, whatever that might be, Bennet really did not know. But his mind was too preoccupied with the new intelligence he had just received and the sickening thought that his wife, Claudia might have been chaste and innocent after all, filled him with an uneasy feeling, almost as if a rodent was gnawing at his very bowels and he felt sick.

It was a bright Saturday morning. The Indians living in the barracks saw themselves as one large family. They gathered at the local temple where turbaned men with colourful dhotis and adorned with streaks of red, yellow and white powder thumped and beat their drums to the rhythm of a cacophony of voices singing in the Eastern dialect. All attention, however, was focussed on Siva, the village fool, who was in the process of executing a dance in a state of trance.

Siva was never taken seriously by the village folk. He was always at the centre of their jokes. But this day was different; nobody indulged in the usual fun at his expense. They were all viewing him with serious faces as he gritted his teeth and clamped his jaws, while extending his arms stiffly with clenched fists, as he danced like one in a state of trance. He goggled and swivelled his eyeballs, whilst he grimly surveyed his surroundings. And then with a shriek, he leapt into the air, displaying energy quite unlike his usual passive self. Even the boldest took a step back. While he swayed and cavorted to the rhythm of the drums, a large goat with a dappled, tan and white coat, was being prepared by a group of men for sacrifice according to the religious rites. This activity was taking place in an elevated area just in front of the temple. The wretched animal was being decorated with yellow and red powder as it bleated piteously. While a man held the goat still with a short rope fastened around its neck, another dressed with only a yellow *dhoti* and naked from waist upwards, held a large silvery moon-shaped knife which glistened in the morning sun. The knife was poised treacherously, a hand's length above the slender neck of the goat. The man focussed his attention on the point of the vertebra, where the knife was expected to slice through cleanly, to separate the head from the body in one precise stroke. The goat continued to bleat unremittingly, almost as if it knew its fate. In a flash of silvery steel, the knife came down and the head separated. Thick, warm arterial blood spurted out to form a fountain as the goat kicked spasmodically.

The crowd was momentarily distracted from Siva as all heads were turned in the direction of the beheaded goat. If anyone had taken an interest in Siva at that moment, they would have noticed, an almost imperceptible change in his countenance, as he too swivelled his head in the general direction of the new attraction. It took him only a few seconds to realise that he was no longer the centre of interest. Even the drummers were distracted though they continued to beat the drums, without any visible signs of a break in the rhythm. Siva regained his composure and pranced towards the goat that was still kicking in the final throes of death as its life slowly ebbed away. The drummers increased their beats and followed Siva. It was only when he knelt at the hind legs of the animal and reached out towards the forelegs that his intention became known: he wanted to manoeuvre the carcass in order to direct the pulsating blood into his gaping mouth, to demonstrate the virility of the spirit, with which he was possessed. But all did not go as planned. The goat, which appeared to have been dead, kicked spasmodically in the final throes of death. Not expecting such a thrust from a "dead" goat, Siva's resistance was low. He rolled down the slope, amidst gut wrenching, belly wobbling laughter and tears. The drummers, too laughed, but they played on. But Siva was not done. He pranced up the slope and this time approached the carcass more cautiously, avoiding the rear legs, and picked it up to allow the remaining warm blood to dribble into his mouth. His face splattered with blood, he looked hideously gory as he continued to sway to the rhythm of the drums.

The village folk were thoroughly enjoying the day. They participated passionately in the cultural and religious activities; they loved the side attractions which they found thoroughly entertaining; they were in the company of people they loved and enjoyed and most of all there were food aplenty. But Chandra cut a desolate figure as he stood alone. It had been three days since he had confronted Baigum. Although both still shared the same roof, they had not spoken to each other since the confrontation. They continue to engage in the routine daily chores, but in silence. The only sounds now were that of their little girl who engaged them in her play with her dolls.

His mood was sombre and conspicuously out of step with the spirit of the day. Nobody attempted to join him. He did not hear the laughter, the drum beats and the multitude of voices that surrounded him, neither did he take an interest in the activities around him. He mulled over the events of the past few days—playing them them over and over in his mind. It was not getting any better. Speculative stories of Claudia Bennet's murder, Mathuray's death and the fact that he was a witness abounded in the village. His unexpected and sudden rise to the position of a *sirdar* and now the impending threat of his fall from grace with the Bennets were common knowledge. He found himself surrounded by circumstances that gnawed at his very soul. He was a troubled man.

He seldom reminisced about India and the family he had left behind. Even the memory of Shubnum had faded away like clouds sailing away in a current of air. But now he found it comforting as he sought refuge in her memory. He thought of the times when they used to steal away for several hours on the lake with the flat bottom boat. He knew that his family would be furious but he used to placate them with a healthy catch of river fish. At other times they would lie on the bank of the river looking into the sky and identifying the many shapes of the clouds; sometimes it would be a face of an old woman which morphed into woolly sheep, at other times they took the form of a tiger or a bird. But they never failed to recognise some shape or another, always. At times they would look deeply into the blue of the sky and watch swallows weaving loops within loops and they would vicariously enjoy the thrill of riding the air currents effortlessly on spread wings.

He did not realise it but it was already past midday and the crowd was starting to thin. He felt weary and weak as he made his way back to his cottage.

John Bennet was restless. His mind was in a turmoil as he vacillated between intense feelings of guilt for having killed his wife and his primeval sense of survival: he had to protect himself from being exposed as the one who had murdered his wife. More importantly he had to do everything possible to preserve and protect his relationship with his son.

In the mornings when his head was heavy with the after-effects of the previous night's drunkenness, he felt vulnerable and weak and sank into the depths of despondency. It was at these times that he would cry and whimper softly with remorse and it was at these times that he would reach out for any hard liquor that he could lay his hands on. And as the liquid burnt its way, comfortingly down his throat, he would undergo a miraculous transformation—he was in control once again. He resolved to confront the Coolie who had been responsible for much of his woes. After having downed a fair amount of brandy, sitting at a table in the open portico along the side of the house under a thatched roof, he felt that the problems were not so bad after all. No one was going to believe a coolie and *he* was a white man; the Laws of the Country were there to protect white people. Coolies were nothing more than slaves—well maybe a slight compromise between the free market system and slavery. But he was John Bennet! And no problem was too big to handle. "Tembi!" he bellowed. Tembi, whose cottage was barely fifty paces away, opened her door and poked her head out curiously. "Tembi!' he bellowed again. Tembi shuffled out of the cottage and waddled across with her ample bosom bouncing with every step.
Bennet's command of the African language Zulu was commendable.
"I want you to call that coolie . . . . what's his name? Chan . . . Chan . . . ."
"Chaandra?" interjected Tembi, giving the name a strange twist, peculiar to her dialect.

"Yes! Chandra!" replied Bennet. "Tell him I want to see him—now!"

Despite the fact that Tembi had been working for the Bennets for over a decade, her eyes never failed to widen with fear every time she was in the presence of John Bennet.

Wiping her face with the edge of her apron, she responded with a hasty "Yes Baas!" and scurried away to do his bidding.

Chandra was busy in the little garden patch in which mealie plants and a few essential vegetables were thriving. These days he preferred spending long hours in the garden; here, he found temporary refuge from the anxieties of the recent developments. On seeing Tembi, he stopped working and leaned on the handle of the hoe with both his hands. Tembi used a mixture of Zulu and hand gestures to communicate that John Bennet wished to see him. He had been dreading this day but he knew it was inevitable. His anger towards Baigum surfaced all over again. He knew that he was being summoned by John Bennet to answer to the allegation that he had revealed information to the villagers. While he knew he was innocent, the frustration of not being able to find a plausible explanation for the stories abounding in the village, worried him. Had Baigum, perhaps, unwittingly divulged the information to someone? John Bennet would never believe his innocence. On the other hand, perhaps he should rightfully be held responsible for the present state of affairs; had he not divulged the secret to Baigum, this crisis would not have existed. Chandra's mind was preoccupied with these thoughts as he washed his hands and face with water collected from the river. Baigum was busy with the cooking and his daughter was asleep on the floor when he left for Bennet's cottage.

Chandra found John Bennet in the open portico seated at the table with a half empty bottle of brandy. His face had an oily sheen to it. His eyes had a fiery glare. He did not utter a word as Chandra stepped up onto the portico. Chandra clasped his hat respectfully against his chest with both his hands and bowed subserviently. Bennet noticed that Chandra's general demeanour was conspicuously different from his behaviour the last time he had met him—when Chandra had negotiated his position of *sirdar*. The arrogance and confidence he had exuded then had now disappeared. Bennet could sense it. But he knew that he had to handle this man with all the cunning at his disposal. He was alert to the fact that he could not allow himself to succumb to the pleasure of extracting vengeance. Bennet had already made up his mind that Chandra had been responsible for the stories abounding in every household in the area. But he knew that there was still a chance that he could get this man to convince his son that he was innocent.

"*Sahib*, you sent for me?" Chandra enquired to escape the uncomfortable silence.

"So you have been spreading these malicious and false stories about me?"

"*Sahib*?"

"You understand me! You have been saying bad things about me!" Bennet saw the need to simplify his language to accommodate the Indian.

"*Sahib*! I say nothing!" protested Chandra pathetically.

"Then how is it that people are talking? How is it that my son also believes this story?"

"*Sahib*, I donno!" whimpered Chandra pathetically. Clearly, both men were fighting for their survival: Bennet was fighting to protect his relationship with his son and stay out of jail while Chandra was struggling to retain his position as *sirdar*. Despite the promise to himself to handle this man with a cool cunning he lost his composure, though momentarily. He slammed the table with the side of his fist The table shuddered and the goblet from which he had been drinking crashed to the floor, splintering into many pieces. The brandy bottle danced precariously with the vibration of the table. Bennet steadied the bottle with one hand as he stood up to reach for Chandra with the other. Chandra impulsively stepped out of reach as Bennet blubbered incoherently; spittle from Bennet speckled the table. He realised that any chance of salvaging his relationship with his son would be compromised if he lost his hold over the Indian. Since Claude was going to engage with the Indian, and the Indian would reveal the truth, if he had nothing to lose, Bennet checked himself and resumed his seat.

"Alright! Let me listen to you!" Bennet forced an uneasy smile.

Chandra, noticing the change in temperament, ventured to approach the table, though somewhat suspiciously.

"*Sahib!* I tell no one!" Chandra's voice took on a tone of conspiratorial whisper.

"Then please tell me how it has got to this! Did you tell your wife?"

Chandra did not answer but cast his eyes down; he found that he could not look at Bennet in the eye. This did not escape Bennet.

"So you told your wife!" Chandra affirmed this with an almost indiscernible nod of his head. Bennet looked down and rubbed his eyes with his forefinger and thumb while he calculated his next move. Bennet reasoned that there was still a chance that he could use this Indian to salvage the situation; he realised that his entire life hinged on the testimony of this man and he knew that he had to resort to craft and cunning to survive.

"So my son has not spoken to you as yet?" a fact that he had already known but mentioned it to ease into the demands that he had already formulated in his head.

"You did not see me on that day in question! You don't know anything! You have not met with me today! Do you understand me?"

"*Sahib!* I understand! I donno anything!"

"Now go!" Bennet recharged his glass as he leaned forward to rest his elbows on the table.

Chandra made his way back to the cottage. Although he knew that he was not out of the woods yet, he felt relieved that he was not removed from his position as *sirdar* for that was his worst fear and that was what he had expected when he was summoned by Bennet.

He felt somewhat at ease for the first time in many days. Although he was acutely sensitive to the fact that Claude Bennet was bound to question him about the purported rumour about his father's involvement in his mother's murder, he took solace in the fact that he had won the round with the lion and dealing with the cub would be less of a problem.

Although the relationship between Baigum and himself had been strained, with very little communication between them, she had continued to discharge all her obligations as a good Indian wife would. When he reached the cottage, she was preparing his favourite meal of *dholl* and cabbage. His daughter was peering through the window at a butterfly. He found it easier to slip into a mood of conciliation now that he felt less threatened.

It is strange and yet it plays itself out daily in every sphere of life irrespective of religious, social or economic groups; man's reaction to every external stimuli is based on the fundamental emotion of either love or fear. Chandra's anger with Baigum was essentially based on fear. He was afraid of the potential threat to his social and economic status—hence his reaction towards Baigum, whom he suspected was responsible for his current woes. Now that he seemed to have secured his position as *sirdar*, he was more amenable towards mending his relationship with his wife. Yet, the issue of whether Baigum had, indeed, divulged information to a third party had not been resolved in his mind.

His daughter, Parvathy, extended her arms inviting him to carry her. He scooped her up and took his usual place on the wooden chair at the table. He kissed her fondly on the forehead as she offered her rag doll, expecting her father to give it some attention too. Chandra welcomed this as it temporarily relieved him of the uncomfortable silence between himself and Baigum. Although he knew what was being prepared for the evening meal, he still enquired in order to start a conversation'

"What are you cooking?" he asked.

"Dal and cabbage!" she replied, taking note of the change in mood and temperament.

"That's nice! I'm hungry!" he added.

"I still have my job as a sirdar," he continued.

Baigum made the connection; the change in attitude could only be attributed to his securing his position as *sirdar*.

"Do you still believe that I am responsible for spreading the story of Sahib Bennet?" she asked, removing the end of the sarie which she used to cover her face, for the first time.

"That is not important now!" he replied

"I need to know! It is important to me!" she insisted.

"You must understand that I was upset and angry! My position as sirdar hinges around the secrecy and the confidentiality of that fact. If everybody knows then I do not have a hold on Bennet or the position." His daughter agitated to be released from his lap.

"I would rather have had you as a worker like everybody else and live in the barracks like everybody else and travelled on foot like everybody else and your integrity unblemished!" He noticed the confidence, the authority and the touch of defiance with which she said it. The meek and subservient role, characteristic of most Indian wives, appeared to have evaporated.

"But can you not see that I did it for us—for you and Parvathy? Everything I did, I did for us!" For the first time he found himself defending himself without realising it. The child stood looking at them anxiously, sensing the tension between her parents.

"I want the Chandra I knew! You have changed! I want the man who cared for everybody else first before he considered himself; I want the man who was honest, good and kind! Where is he?" Her eyes glistened

with wetness; a tear drop which hung precariously at the tip of her eye lash, began rolling down her cheek. Chandra got up from his seat. His heart melted. He wanted to embrace her and tell her that he was sorry; he wanted to ask her to forgive him; he wanted to tell her that he was still the same man; he wanted to tell her that he had lost his way; he wanted to fold her in his arms and tell her that he loved her and wanted to make amends; instead he unlatched the door and stepped out into the midday sun. He walked slowly, looking hunched as he followed the narrow footpath, not knowing where he was going.

The next day Chandra reported to the fields in his usual manner on horseback but he carried no whip. The absence of the whip was conspicuous and the field workers noticed it and whispered in conspiratorial tones. The aloofness and arrogance seemed to have disappeared; he looked weary. He usually rode across the field just to stamp his authority in order to ensure good conduct for the rest of the day. But on this day he just took his usual place in the shade of a tree while his horse grazed lazily nearby. An hour into the day, he was still sitting there when his peripheral vision picked up a movement in the distance. A single horseman approached. He recognised the familiar figure of Claude Bennet making his way towards him. It was the moment that he had been dreading. But there was a part of him that wanted this meeting to take place so that he would be over it. Very often the stresses, strains and anxieties of an impending confrontation are more unpleasant and debilitating than the confrontation itself. Perhaps, then he would be able to make attempts to repair the damage to his relationships, not only with his wife but with the village folks as well. But his heart was pounding in his rib cage like a galloping horse.

Claude reached Chandra and slid off his horse while still holding on to the reins.

"We need to talk," said Claude with a sense of urgency.

"Yes! Sir!" responded Chandra.

"I believe you have been spreading stories about my father! I need to hear it from you!" said Claude while trying to still his horse which agitated to join the mare grazing lazily nearby.

"*Sahib*! I see nothing! I tell nothing! Where story come from — I donno!" responded Chandra.

Claude was relieved to hear this from the man whom the villagers claimed was the source of the offensive and incriminating bit of information. But as much as he wanted to accept the *coolie's* word and walk away, happy in the knowledge that his father was innocent, he had to make sure in order to put this matter to rest. What if the coolie was lying? He knew that if there was any truth in the stories it would be devastatingly disastrous for the future of the Bennets.

Nobody noticed Rathnam who, on seeing Claude speaking to Chandra, made his way closer to the men, to be within earshot of the exchange between them.

"But everybody says that you saw my father on the morning when my mother was killed and that my father had given you the job as *sirdar* to keep you quiet," Claude probed and waited. There was an uncomfortable momentary silence before Chandra responded.

"Sir! People don't like me! They make trouble! I am good worker. I don't steal, I work hard and I am clever! *Sahib* call me and say I must be *sirdar*!"

Rathnam may not have heard every word but he had heard enough to realise that Chandra was desperately scrambling to keep his future intact. But Rathnam knew that Chandra's future as a man of authority was hanging at the end of a thread of gossamer. While he feigned to be engrossed with cutting the cane with his sickle, no one noticed a glimmer of a smile spread across his face.

Indecision and uncertainty can be a source of stress and anxiety even though the options presented may not be detrimental to the individual taking the decision. Rathnam found himself in such a position. He was armed with vital information but how to use the information to ensure maximum results bothered him. His original objective to ensure that Chandra toppled from grace with the Bennets and to see him grovelling in the ranks of an ordinary field labourer, was fuelled by an intense and burning hatred for Chandra—the man who had not only usurped his position of *sirdar* but the one who had also humiliated him. Despite the passage of at least six months his hatred was as intense as ever and he thought, how much sweeter his vengeance would be if Chandra fell from grace and he, Rathnam reclaimed the position of *sirdar*. He pondered the risks and the gains of all the possible options. If he approached John Bennet then he would be exposing himself as the one who had spread the story; that would be detrimental to his own welfare. Claude Bennet, on the other hand, was driven by a moral compulsion to establish the truth. But the truth would destroy his family. It was not likely that Claude Bennet would look kindly upon the bearer of such information. Such was the dilemma facing Rathnam. He slept very little as he pondered and mulled over his next move and then with a spark of realisation, the clouds cleared. His ambition and desire were less important. Ensuring that Chandra paid for the suffering and humiliation was of paramount importance in the interest of his own psychological health. His pathological obsession for revenge could be remedied only with the fall of Chandra.

Although Rathnam was no longer the *sirdar* he was still able to exert a fair amount of influence amongst the field workers who remembered his tenure as the *sirdar*. In fact, Chandra's aggressive style of overseeing had elevated Rathnam's image amongst the labourers who preferred him over Chandra as a *sirdar*. Rathnam had little problem in convincing, Veetu, a female indentured labourer of dubious reputation that Chandra was extremely susceptible to the amorous attention of women, especially now that the relationship between Chandra and his wife was strained. The uneasy peace between Chandra and Baigum was common knowledge in the barracks community. Of course, Rathnam did not fail to mention the benefits that she would enjoy if Chandra compromised himself with her.

Veetu was no more than twenty five years old. Her pretty doll-like face and her jet black hair, neatly parted in the centre and rolled into a bun was an attraction for the men. She complemented this by pulling her sarie taut over her body, quite unlike the other women who draped their saries loosely in keeping with the demands of the tradition and culture. Men were comfortable in engaging in ribaldry with her and she was not averse to it. So when Rathnam approached her to seduce Chandra, she was quite intrigued with the prospect of the challenge to exploit the sexual weakness of a person in authority. In fact, she found it to be strangely and fetishly erotic.

Chandra was quite perplexed and thought that it was outrageously impudent when Veetu approached him one afternoon while he was seated, resting against a tree. She offered to massage him and justified the rather unusual offer by pointing out that he looked exhausted at the end of the day's work and that he deserved some pampering. Most men would have welcomed such a gesture as an opening and an invitation to explore and sample what was being offered. Chandra stared at her, wide eyed in bewilderment. How should he react to such a strange request that was clearly beyond the bounds of acceptable behaviour? He was acutely aware of the fact that he should not do or say anything that would compromise his authority as a *sirdar*. He had not developed a construct to cope with the situation confronting him and clearly, he was stressed. Man by nature will always react in such a manner so as to remove any source of stress and restore the equilibrium of his psychological make-up. Right now Veetu was a source of stress. So, despite the sexual attraction, he had a sense of foreboding and reacted spontaneously and impulsively.

"Woman! You have the impudence and the audacity to offer your services to me. Do you not have any shame?

Veetu, who had not expected such a response, was taken aback.

"I was only trying to be nice. Your wife is not fulfilling that function right now!"

The statement cut deep and Chandra winced.

"Do you not have any respect for yourself and the fact that I belong to another?"

Somehow the proprietorial reference rang hollow, for the uneasy strain in his relationship with Baigum was uppermost in his mind.

"Now be gone with you!" he barked and Veetu, who was generally accustomed to the ribaldry and the lewd attention she evoked in men, felt disconcerted and more than just a little embarrassed. She walked away amidst sniggering from the women on the field and lewd comments from the men and she was hot with fury.

Rathnam was disappointed that Chandra had not succumbed to Veetu's sexual overtures. The months had not diluted his intense dislike for the man and in a twisted and diabolical way this hatred had given him something to look forward to. All his thoughts hinged around Chandra's ultimate downfall. He calculated and planned to bring about Chandra's fall from grace. His ultimate objective was to get Chandra to lose his position as a *sirdar*, to cause dissension in his family life and to deprive him of material comforts. What set Chandra apart from the others, in a material sense, were his cottage that was allocated to him and his mode of transport.

It was therefore not surprising when he sneaked out of his barracks quarters in the dark of a wintry evening, armed with a pick and a spade. He walked stealthily, slightly hunched, as one who wanted to remain obscure and unseen. The night was extremely dark; he could barely see his hand before his face but he was familiar with the terrain. He walked for about twenty minutes before he stopped. His eyes had grown accustomed to the darkness and he was able to see better. He felt the bite of the cold breeze and he shuddered involuntarily. He dropped the spade on the slightly damp ground and it fell with a low thud in the silence of the night. He felt the ground with his bare toes to establish where he should start digging. Before long he felt warm with the activity as he struck the ground repeatedly with the pick. He worked feverishly, loosening the soil with the pick and removing it with the spade. In less than an hour he had dug a knee-deep trench across the rutted road. He then proceeded to fill the trench with leaves from the sugar cane plantation which flanked the road on either side. But he ensured that the leaves were just enough to support a layer of soil. Although it was dark, he had done a fairly good job and no casual observer would have noticed that the ground was tampered with. He gathered his tools and hurried back to his quarters with the feeling of a poacher who had just set a trap. All he had to do now was wait.

The relationship between Chandra and Baigum was still steeled with cold tension. The usual small talk, the exchange of smiles, the loving touch were absent. They spoke on a needs basis. Even their usual jocular engagement with their little daughter ceased. But they discharged their commitments dutifully. She kept the house neat and tidy and cooked and ensured that he had his meals on time He reported to work and ensured that Baigum and his daughter were not deprived of any material comforts that he could provide. On this morning, Baigum handed him the white enamel cup with the usual hot tea made from fresh cow's milk. He finished his tea, set the cup on the table and wiped his mouth with the back of his hand as he stepped out of the house to saddle his mare. The morning sky was tinged with streaks of red as the sun peeked above the blanket of green foliage of uncut cane in the eastern horizon. The horse blinked at him with rheumy eyes from behind the gate of the makeshift stable. The smell of horse dung and hay attracted flies which buzzed around him, but he was accustomed to this. He threw the saddle across the horse's back and fastened the straps. He held the horn of the saddle and hoisted himself easily onto it. He felt good as he eased himself into the moulded hollow of the saddle. He nudged the horse with his heel and it set off on a slow trot. The narrow foot trail merged into a wider rutted wagon track. The mare broke into a slow canter without any prompts from Chandra. He always allowed it to follow its natural urge as it increased its speed to almost a gallop. He too, loved the physical exertion and found it refreshingly exhilarating. This day was no different. Though the air was cold and the breeze created by the swift gallop nipped at his earlobes, it did not bother him. The road ahead stretched for more than a mile before it curved gently to the left. This is where the mare loved to increase its pace to full gallop and Chandra stood on the stirrups and hoisted himself slightly off the saddle to give it advantage. For a brief moment he did not think of the tension in his relationship with Baigum, he did not think of his image in the community nor did he think of the precarious nature of his position as a *sirdar*—for now it was just himself, the horse and the road. About three hundred yards ahead there was slight evidence of the ground having been recently unearthed. This could not be evident to a casual observer. There was no chance of the horse and rider detecting this. He had no time to think as the solid feel of the horse and saddle below him gave way in full stride. He heard a distinct crack like that of a dry twig breaking as he found himself airborne and plunging forward ahead of the horse. His face made contact with the cobbled surface with a sickening thud as the momentum propelled him along the ground, scraping the skin off his face and hands. He was numbed with shock. He did not feel the burning sensation of the raw and angry abrasion on his face nor the pain of his body as he turned around in response to the high pitched screams of the horse. Its forelegs were in a trench as it lay on its side. It tried to lift itself out but in vain— its right foreleg appeared to be limp and misaligned. It snorted pitifully with the rims of its nostrils flaring and closing with every agonised breath. Chandra just stared helplessly until he gathered his thoughts and stepped into the trench to examine the horse's injury. Its leg had already swollen and it resisted Chandra's attempt at examining the extent of its injury. The dreadful reality that the horse had broken its leg dawned on him. She tried to lift herself again but collapsed helplessly snorting with pain and lay on its side. Chandra did not realise it but he was trembling.

Soon a small group of field workers gathered around the horse, chattering among themselves and a few of the bolder and more senior men attempted to offer suggestions as to what should be done. Chandra had grown to accept that he was alone. Over the months the village folk and the barrack's community had stayed away from him. He had lost his reputation as a leader and a man who cared for his people. His ruthlessness in imposing his authority as a *sirdar* and the dubiousness surrounding the acquisition of his position was common knowledge and he had become accustomed to being ostracised by the village folk. He therefore felt ill at ease and awkward when the men offered their assistance. The consequences and implications of his horse's injury stared him starkly in the face — the horse had to be shot. One of the men offered to go to the Bennet's household. Claude Bennet rode in within twenty minutes. Most of the Indians had left to report to the fields. Claude Bennet slid down from his horse and went into the trench where the horse lay and held the hoof of the right leg to examine its injury. The mare protested in agony. Claude climbed out and confirmed the diagnosis. He looked at Chandra and noticed the severe abrasions on his face.

"We need to attend to you! Meet me at the cottage," he said.

"The horse, *Sahib*?" enquired Chandra, still looking distraught and shaken.

"The horse must be shot!" replied Claude.

Although Chandra saw the horse as a material asset, the loss of which would have implications for his convenience and he believed, for his status as well, it now evoked an emotion that he never knew he had. When Claude mentioned that the horse had to be shot, the finality of this announcement sent his mind spinning back to the many, many hours he had spent with the mare and he realised that the horse was more than a material possession and that it had become a companion to him. He still entertained a hope that the horse could be saved with medical intervention and help. The mare tried to lift herself again but groaned pitifully as she collapsed on her side. She looked at Chandra dolefully, blinked its rheumy eyes and bobbed its head almost as if she understood that it was the end. Claude reached for the double barrelled shotgun strapped to the side of his saddle but hesitated momentarily and appeared to have changed his mind; instead he reached for the Smith & Wesson cartridge revolver holstered at his right hip. He slipped the barrel open with a smart flick of the wrist and inspected the chambers and was satisfied that the revolver was fully loaded. Claude had not done this before but he had observed his father at least on three occasions. He stepped in front of the horse, cocked the hammer and pointed the revolver a hand's length from its forehead and waited for a reasonable pause for it to stay still. Chandra chose to turn away and he waited; he could not bear to look. And then the silence of the morning exploded with a single shot. A flock of large birds took flight amidst a rustling of wings. Chandra turned around slowly and the revolver in Claude's hand was still smoking.

———————

Whether Claude Bennet chose not to pay any heed to the stories among the villagers that his father had been responsible for his mother's death, because he did not believe them, or whether he did not want to face the unpleasantness of the consequences of pursuing such allegations, one will never know. He never approached his father again but the relationship between them was cold. It was becoming increasingly clear that John Bennet was losing his grip on life; he was drunk from dawn till dusk and he neglected his usual routine responsibilities. The farmhands did not see him for days on end; they saw Claude Bennet more often in place of his father. The workers welcomed the change and many of them held a respectful adoration for him. Claude, on the other hand, was very unlike his father. He was compassionate and often displayed a Solomonic wisdom in dealing with and arbitrating in disputes. In fact, they had a newfound enthusiasm for work and Claude had found that productivity had increased, though marginally.

Unlike his father, he refused to dock the wages, as was the general pattern, when workers failed to report to work. But he ensured that he established conclusively that the absence was due to reasons that were valid. He never carried a whip when he visited the fields and workers never failed to greet him with spontaneous enthusiasm as he passed them on horseback. On the rare occasions that John Bennet did visit the field, more as a perfunctory gesture, he failed to intimidate the field labourers as he used to—he appeared drunk and slovenly and lacked the aggressive energy to wield his influence. During these visits, both John and Claude Bennet did not acknowledge the presence of Chandra as a *sirdar*. This was unusual as employers generally consulted with the *sirdars* and issued instructions through them; but this was not the case. Chandra felt the avoidance acutely and it worried him. Workers too noticed the indifference of their bosses towards the *sirdar*. While most of them were unconcerned and apathetic some had a feeling of smug satisfaction to see Chandra being treated with what they perceived as disdain by their employers. Rathnam, on the other hand, was inwardly elated to see Chandra in such dismal circumstances but he ensured that he displayed a cool exterior in keeping with the noncommittal attitude of others. It had been just over a week since the unfortunate incident that had destroyed Chandra's horse. While it was conclusively established that the incident was *not* an accident but the result of a premeditated act intended to injure both horse and rider, the identity of the perpetrator was speculative. Rathnam was the chief suspect given the history of deep bitterness and rivalry between Chandra and himself but there was no evidence linking him to the crime. When approached by Claude Bennet at the behest of Chandra who felt intuitively that Rathnam was responsible for the digging of the trench that maimed his horse, Rathnam denied it vehemently, pointing out that Chandra's standing in the community was by no means a healthy one and that he had made several enemies along the way; he argued that this had widened the probabilities of the identity of the perpetrator. No one could argue the logic of the argument and Rathnam had artfully deflected attention from him—at least for the moment. He therefore went to great lengths to ensure that there were no overt displays of elation at Chandra's misfortune.

Chandra, on the other hand, lacked the aggressive confidence that was characteristic of his manner of supervision. He no longer carried his whip and now that he had no horse, he walked to the field. He was not always present as he had to divide his attention between the two farms, the erstwhile Croft farm and the original Bennet farm. And now that productivity had increased under the wisdom and guidance of Claude Bennet, Chandra had fewer reasons to keep a close watch on the workers. This too, worried him. Was he becoming dispensable? But he continued to report to the fields dutifully every day, took his usual place under the tree, walked around occasionally and exchanged a word or two in terms of progress but did not engage in any overt reprimand of any sort.

He was quite surprised when Rathnam approached him while he was seated one morning at his usual place. Rathnam held his hat against his chest and assumed a slightly hunched position as an ostentatious display of respect, despite the deep animosity between them and addressed him in Hindi.

"The Sahib wants to see you."

"When?" enquired Chandra, who was a little perplexed and concerned that the message was being conveyed through Rathnam.

"This morning!" replied Rathnam.

"How did you get this message?" queried Chandra who really wanted to probe to establish whether there was anything sinister in the fact that it was Rathnam who was the bearer of the message.

"The small Sahib," referring to Claude Bennet, *"came in yesterday afternoon when you were not here!"* replied Rathnam. Chandra felt a little relieved on hearing this but the fact that he was being summoned by John Bennet did not bode well.

Whether John Bennet was drunk or sober was not a pertinent issue anymore; he was always drunk. Even Claude knew that he had to consider the *degree* of drunkenness if he had to have any meaningful interaction with his father. So when Chandra called at the cottage John Bennet was not sober — but he was not debilitatingly drunk. He had the look reserved for the Indians — he appeared morose and truculent. He was seated under the portico of the cottage at the table. A tumbler with a mixture of brandy and water stood next to a bottle of partially consumed brandy. Chandra stepped cautiously onto the stoep. He knew that he was vulnerable and he could not help feeling a cloying sense of anxiety. Bennet picked up the tumbler while he continued to stare above the rim at Chandra. Chandra felt uneasy.

"*Sahib* you call me?" queried Chandra, standing a respectful distance from him. Bennet placed the tumbler on the table and stood up slowly and deliberately. He walked a few paces towards Chandra.

"I want you to vacate your cottage!" Bennet spoke softly. His eyes were mere slits in his face which showed the ravages of excessive drinking; it appeared puffed and more crimson than usual.

"*Sahib?*" Chandra did not seem to understand the import of the statement. Bennet was surprisingly calm. Every one of man's negative emotions is driven fundamentally by fear. Anger too, which can lead to rage, is driven by fear. John Bennet did not feel threatened by Chandra any more. He felt he was in control again because he knew that he was in a position of strength.

"I want you to leave the cottage with your family. I want you to occupy the barracks!" Bennet spoke slowly and deliberately like one trying to communicate with a person who is hard of hearing.

Chandra felt his world collapsing around him.

"*Sahib!* I am the *sirdar!*" protested Chandra.

"Not anymore, you 're not!" said Bennet with smug satisfaction.

"*Sahib!* You cannot do this!" Chandra felt his heart pounding.

"I *am* the master or have you forgotten? I shall do as I please!"

Chandra had never seen Bennet smile, let alone laugh. But Bennet smiled—the kind of smile that never reaches the eyes and then he burst into laughter—a maniacal laughter that echoed through the cottage. And he stopped just as suddenly and his face morphed into a scowl.

"And I suppose you are going to run to the Protector!" Another paroxysm of laughter followed. It was common knowledge that the Protector of Indian Immigrants never offered any protection to the many Indians who were maltreated, abused and exploited. If anything, the title was a misnomer. Bennet was clearly taking refuge in this. But despite his vulnerability and the intimidation from Bennet, Chandra had no intention of succumbing easily to him.

"I not leave. I still the *sirdar!*" Bennet did not expect any resistance from a *coolie*, let alone Chandra. He looked at him, his eyebrows raised and taken aback and his bearded face turned crimson with rage. He lunged at him with open palm in an effort to strike him across the face. Bennet was a big man, a whole head taller than Chandra. Chandra bent low and Bennet's hand swished cleanly above Chandra's head. Bennet's reflexes were too slow to change direction. His forearm thudded painfully against the wooden pole supporting the thatched roof of the portico. Chandra backed away desperately trying to avoid the hostile, physical confrontation with Bennet. But Bennet was not done yet. He lumbered forward, growling with rage.

"*Sahib!* Please . . ." Chandra was not able to complete his plea. Bennet had changed his stance. He now balled his fist and hurled a punch at Chandra's face. Chandra was just in time to tilt his head and he failed to land a full-blooded strike. Bennet was momentarily off-balance and Chandra seized the opportunity to make his way down the stoep. He did not see Bennet trying to scurry after him. He did not see Bennet stumble at the stoep nor did he see him fall. He did not know that his head had struck a beam and that a protruding nail had buried itself almost a finger length into his temple. Tembi, the house-maid, poked her head out of her cottage to see what the commotion was all about and she saw Chandra disappear around the corner. Tembi found Bennet at the foot of the stoep. A thin stream of blood pooled around blades of grass and soaked greedily into the soil. Bennet's eyelids fluttered as he kicked spasmodically scarring the earth with his booted feet.

When Chandra reached his cottage, Baigum had just returned from the river with the day's washing and Parvathy was asleep on a cushion of leaves on the floor. She looked curiously at him for she was not accustomed to having him at home at that part of the day but she said nothing; the relationship between them was still strained.

"The Sahib wants us to leave the cottage!" he said in Hindi and waited for a response. Baigum continued to clean the rice and there was a prolonged, uneasy silence before she spoke.

"Why should we move?" she asked, pretending to be engrossed in the cleaning of the rice.

"He says that I am no longer the sirdar!" Chandra sat on the wooden bench, cradling his head as he stared at the floor.

"I may not approve of the manner in which you acquired the position but I know that you were a good sirdar! I know that you were loyal to him." She said.

"I have lost my friends, I have lost the respect of my fellow-men. I have lost my peace since the day I got this position and I feel that I have even lost you."

She raised her head for the first time and looked at him. She wanted him to embrace her and tell her that he believed in her and that they could weather the storms together. He looked at her and her eyes were moist and a tear dribbled down her cheek. He stood up and extended his hand and she rushed towards him. He folded her in a warm embrace. Parvathy, who was asleep on the floor awoke and tottered groggily towards her father. Chandra scooped her up with his arm still around Baigum. He jiggled her playfully to get her attention. The child yawned sleepily while rubbing her eyes with her little knuckles. For the moment he forgot about his misfortunes and felt wanted and loved and realised how much they meant to him; he realised then that his status and position were not as important as loving and protecting his little girl and his wife. He knew that with them at his side he would be able to survive the loss of his position as *sirdar* and withstand the loss of the material comforts of life. But how was he to know that losing his position as *sirdar* and losing his cottage would pale into insignificance against what lay ahead.

News of Bennet's death spread through the village within hours. Claude who had been out of town, negotiating for a new plough, returned to see a small crowd of people around his cottage. The local constabulary was also there. Sergeant Greene and Constable Barney were questioning Tembi, the maid, who had seen Chandra leaving the cottage. Tembi was holding the edge of her apron to cover her mouth as she spoke, her eyes still bulging with shock and fear. When Sergeant Greene noticed Claude approaching them, he turned his attention towards him, while he waved the maid away. When Claude enquired of Sergeant Greene the circumstances surrounding his father's death, he appeared remarkably calm. There appeared to be no doubt in the Sergeant's mind that Chandra had, indeed, killed John Bennet.

Claude could not help feeling guilty that he was not experiencing any sorrow at the sudden demise of his father. In fact, he felt a sense of relief. The question of whether his father had, indeed, been responsible for his mother's death was not resolved in his mind. He found it a matter of expediency not to probe to unravel the truth. So when Chandra denied knowing anything of his father's culpability in his mother's murder, Claude felt relieved and he chose not to pursue the matter any further, although deep within him, the uncertainty and the probability of his father's culpability, affected him deeply. But he knew with sudden realisation that if Chandra was implicated he would reveal the truth if his father was indeed guilty and the reputation of his family would be severely compromised.

••••••••••••••••••••••

Chandra had not left his cottage since his confrontation with Bennet. He had not reported to the field although he knew that John Bennet would deduct two days of wages for every day that he was absent from work; this was common practice amongst the sugar cane barons. He was aware that although Claude Bennet did not practise this, his case would be handled by John Bennet himself.

He had no knowledge of Bennet's death although this was a topic of intense discussion throughout the village. His reunion with Baigum, after months of strain in his relationship, had thrust both of them into the magic of a new romance. They loved it and realised how much they meant to each other. Parvathy too, loved the presence of both the parents together. Despite the impending threat of losing both his position as *sirdar* and the cottage, they took solace in the fact that they were in a committed and loving relationship. They laughed and loved well into the night. At times, the mood changed from a light-hearted banter and Baigum's coquetry to a serious discussion of their future. They discussed the possibility of saving enough money to pay for their passage back to India after their five-year contract expired. They even considered the need for a little brother or sister for Parvathy, who slept soundly on a crude mattress filled with fowl feathers. They watched her fondly as her little chest rose and fell with every breath. But amidst it all there were times when his mind harked back to the memories of Shubnum. He knew that despite his commitment and love for Baigum, Shubnum would always occupy a special niche in his heart. But he was sensitive enough not to mention this to Baigum. If by chance, any reference was made to her, Baigum would artfully steer away from it. But

Chandra's past with Shubnum had never been a cause of any antagonism or bitterness between them. For now, all they wanted was a life together. They felt buoyant and optimistic.

They awoke to the crowing of the cock at four o' clock in the morning. Despite the optimism of the day before, Chandra could not help feeling troubled with a deep sense of foreboding. He knew that he had to face the reality of what lay ahead. Parvathy was still asleep when Baigum got the fire going. She piled in the coal and soon the cottage was filled with a homely warmth. Parvathy stirred, propped herself on her elbow and looked around sleepily. On seeing Chandra, who was seated at the table with a cup of tea in an enamel cup, she ambled over to him with extended arms. He picked her up and nuzzled her lovingly against her forehead and nose. She giggled playfully as he jiggled her on his lap in a mock dance ritual. Outside the dawn was breaking. He would have left an hour earlier but on this day he felt a closeness to his family that he had not felt in a long while. The dread and anxiety of facing the day and the comfort of the home front had him procrastinating every minute.

The knock on the door was startling in the still of the morning. Chandra stood frozen for a moment. He could feel and hear his heart pounding. Baigum suspended her chores and looked towards the door. The rapping on the door startled them again. Even Parvathy looked terrified. Chandra unlatched the door and it was flung open by two men. Sergeant Greene and Constable Barney stood at the door. Constable Barney held a baton which he had used to rap on the door. Chandra was taken by complete surprise when Sergeant Greene stepped in and attempted to wrestle his arm towards his back while the constable dangled a pair of handcuffs with which he attempted to lock Chandra's wrists. But Chandra resisted. He slipped out of the hold with ease using the years of experience in wrestling with the boys at home. When they realised that their task was more difficult than anticipated, Sergeant Greene plucked the baton from the constable and used both his hands to drive it into Chandra's abdomen. With the wind out of him, he was forced to bend over. The sergeant wielded the baton which landed with a dull thud at the back of his head. Chandra slipped silently to the floor and the constable handcuffed his wrists. All this while, Baigum screamed and cried, while Parvathy held onto her mother's sarie, whimpering with fear. Chandra was not conscious when he was loaded into the caged cart drawn by two horses. Clutching the front of her sarie with one hand, and her daughter with the other, Baigum ran after the cart until she could run no more. She watched in bewilderment as the cart disappeared around the bend of the rutted track. She felt alone, so very alone and her body shook with fear and anger.

When Chandra regained consciousness, he found himself in a place that was unpleasantly familiar. The place was dark, save for a panel of light that streamed in through a little barred window, at twice his height on one side of the little enclosure. He felt disorientated and confused and then the stark reality dawned on him. He realised he was in jail. He had seen this place before — but now he was on the other side of the steel bars of the opening that led to the long dim passage. But what was he doing here? He had no answers but he knew that John Bennet had something to do with the present circumstances in which he found himself. The memory of Mathuray clutching the steel bars, begging him to speak to the *sahib*, with tears in his eyes, came flooding back. His thoughts were in a jumble; he thought of Baigum and his little daughter and questioned why this was happening to him. Was this the law of *Karma* playing itself out? He wanted to pray for release from this nightmare but the words of Mathuray rang loudly in his head:

"Where is this God that deems it fit to reward such dedication with this kind of life?"

He was oblivious to the incessant buzzing of the metallic green flies and the strong smell of faeces. In desperation, he called out, *"Sahib! Sahib!"* But all he heard was the dull, hollow echo that mocked him cynically in his desperation.

Baigum had learned from the village folk that Chandra had shoved the *Sahib* down the stoep and that the *Sahib* had fallen and died. But Baigum found it difficult to believe this, as Chandra had given no indication that an incident of this magnitude had taken place, although she was aware of the deep animosity between Chandra and the *Sahib.*

She hurriedly prepared food which she packed into a tin container and with a little water for the road she set off with Parvathy on her six mile walk to the village police station where she knew Chandra was being held. She carried her daughter on her hip in order to increase her pace. The sun had risen just over two hours earlier and she could feel the discomfort of the heat. She realised after a while that she was seriously encumbered by the child in one hand and the cans of food and water in the other. Her body was already aching with the effort and she had a good two hours of distance to cover. When she noticed a patch of shade under a large spreading tree, it was too tempting to ignore. She let Parvathy down with relief and sat, leaning against the trunk of the tree. She was already tired but she knew that she must complete her journey. She realised also with anxiety that she must make her way back and she shuddered at the thought. Parvathy, though only three years old, displayed a maturity beyond her years. Noticing the tears on her mother's cheeks, she wiped it off with her little hands saying in Hindi, *"Don't cry mother! We'll bring father home!"* This only served to exacerbate the dismal circumstances she found herself in. She embraced her little girl and just when she was ready to continue her journey, she noticed that the road, a few paces away had been trenched and hurriedly covered. It dawned on her that, *that* was the spot where Chandra had lost his horse. But she was troubled by the fact that the incident was not the result of a mere accident but a deliberate attempt at destroying Chandra. All this while she had believed that Chandra had lost his horse in an accident. It was the time when their relationship was strained and they had not spoken much. The fact that Chandra was a victim of circumstances perpetrated by individuals with evil, sinister and devious intentions angered her and her heart bled for her husband. She felt guilty that he had gone through so much, for so long and she had not been able to provide the succour and comfort when he needed her the most. She felt a closeness to her husband that filled her with hope and renewed strength. She set off once again with her daughter on her hip.

Her feet ached but she did not stop. At intervals she allowed Parvathy to walk; although it slowed them down, Baigum was able to steal a brief period of relief. In just over two hours she reached the village. She enquired for directions to the police station and an avuncular looking turbaned Indian pointed her in the right direction.

The police station was an inconspicuous looking red brick building. She stepped nervously into the open door. Constable Barney lay slumped in a wooden chair, enjoying a mid-day sleep. The jingle of Baigum's ankle bracelet interrupted his deep sonorous snore. He awoke with a start and reached for his baton, displaying the typical disorientation of one who awakes from a deep sleep. On noticing Baigum, he jumped out of his chair, flattened his hair with the palm of his hand and tugged his collar to look authoritatively dignified. Baigum really did not think of what she was going to say and now she realised that communication was going to be difficult. But Constable Barney had recognised her as the wife of Chandra.

"So you have come to see your husband? he asked with an air of authority. Baigum shook her head in affirmation.

"I'm giving you fifteen minutes!" he said as he led them across a courtyard to a separate building. They walked along a dimly lit passage until they came to an enclosure with steel bars. She noticed Chandra sitting on the floor, in the far corner, clasping his head which was bowed between his knees.

"Chandra!" she called out but she only managed to whisper; her heart was too heavy with despair. Constable Barney used his baton to rattle the bars. Chandra looked up. He saw Baigum and his little girl. He strode over towards them and extended both his arms through the bars to caress them.

Baigum turned around to implore the constable to open the gate to allow them access to each other without the metallic cold bars between them, but Constable Barney had already left and they could hear his footsteps fade away down the passage.

"*How are you?* he asked solemnly while Parvathy reached out between the bars to get his attention.

"*We want you back with us!*" she said with tears streaming down her cheeks.

"*I don't even know why I am here.*"

A mixture of black and grey stubs of beard made him look older than his age.

"*Did they not tell you?*" she enquired with surprise.

"*I was not conscious when they locked me in here. I have not seen anyone. What have I done to deserve this?*" Baigum felt relieved. Her husband was clearly not aware of the charge against him. He must be innocent.

"*The sahib is dead!*" she said.

"*How? I saw him yesterday. He was fit enough to want to attack me!*"

"*Tell me what happened!*" she asked in earnest.

He related the events leading up to the point when he hurried away to escape from Bennet's rage.

"You are being accused of having been responsible for his fall that caused his death." she said between sobs.

"That's not true! When I left him he was very much alive!"

"I know you are innocent. What are we going to do?"

"You must go to the Protector's office." he implored in desperation, although they both knew that given the seriousness of the charge, the Protector would do little or nothing to establish the truth and to resolve the issue to their satisfaction. It was common knowledge that getting to meet with the Protector would be an astronomical task. Subconsciously they were playing out a psychological need to act in order to hang on to hope, however little it might be. But what they did not know was that the Protector was employed to protect the interests of the employer against the transgressions of the Indians employed. Even in the face of blatant maltreatment of Indians by the employers, there was always a leaning in favour of the colonists. Even magistrates were reluctant to pronounce sentences that would compromise the interests of the prosperous sugar barons. The reality, therefore, for the future of Chandra, appeared bleak and dismal.

Twenty minutes had passed and they heard the footsteps of the constable down the passage.

"Time is up!" he said, pointing the baton at Baigum, gesturing her to leave. Parvathy clasped her mother's leg on seeing the constable as she recalled the assault on her father earlier in the day. Baigum felt fearfully anxious and inadequate and Chandra felt helpless. He knew that Baigum did not have the capacity to initiate and execute efforts to prove his innocence and to have him freed. Language was also a barrier. In a flash of hope he thought of Claude Bennet. He was always fair and even-handed. If Baigum could convince him of his innocence there was still a hope for him.

"You have to leave now!" Constable Barney barked and stepped closer to Baigum menacingly.

"Please!" implored Chandra, steepling his palms, "little longer! Please!"

The constable appeared to be indecisive. He was caught between maintaining his authority and the innocent and innocuous nature of the request, which was inconsequential to him or the constabulary. Without appearing to be overtly amenable to the request he scowled and stepped away.

"Go to the little Sahib and tell him the truth. He will understand!" Chandra spoke hurriedly while Constable Barney stood aside, holding his baton and tapping it at timed intervals into the palm of his hand, more as a habit rather than as a show of aggression.

"Go!" said Chandra, *"you have a long way to walk!"* He watched them walk down the long passage. Baigum and Parvathy stopped at the end of the passage and waved; the constable prodded them to move and they disappeared around the bend. *"Do not go too close to the lion, my son! You will not survive the bite!"* The words of his father rang in his head. Chandra held the bars of his prison and his body was racked with emotion; he cried and sobbed unashamedly and the sounds reverberated pitilessly in mocking echoes in the dark.

When Baigum reached her cottage it was late afternoon. She was exhausted. Her body ached; the skin on the soles of her feet had developed little ruptures and appeared crimson and raw. Parvathy had fallen asleep long before she reached the cottage and Baigum was forced to carry her all the way. She let her down on the crude mattress on the floor and cuddled up next to her. She felt the deep void of Chandra's absence. It was not long before her eyelids grew heavy and she lapsed into a long and dreamless sleep. She awoke early the next morning and the events of the day before flooded her mind. Her daughter was still asleep. She felt forlorn and desolate and her heart was heavy with loneliness. But she knew that she must do whatever she could, however small, in order to bring Chandra back home. She felt a moral compulsion to act not only because Chandra was her husband but because he was an innocent man. Their only hope was Claude Bennet. The fact that Claude was known to be fair minded, even-handed and kind, made her feel a little buoyant and optimistic and then her hope crumbled when she thought of Chandra's relationship with the Bennets and the circumstances surrounding his rise to the position of *sirdar*. But she had no idea how she was going to communicate; she had only a smattering of English but she had the determination of a spawning salmon. Leaving Parvathy in the care of the midwife who had delivered her, she set off for Bennet's cottage.

When she reached Bennet's cottage she was not surprised to find that there were many people in and around the house. There was an atmosphere of quiet and solemn activity, in preparation for the funeral. She was nervous and apprehensive. Despite the *Sahib's* reputation for being kind and accommodating she began to have doubts. How would he receive her knowing that her husband was allegedly responsible for his father's death? Clearly, they were in mourning — approaching the *Sahib* now may not elicit the most favourable response. She felt her determination flagging and her anxiety grew deeper. But she knew that she did not have the option of deferring the interaction with him. There was no telling what the consequences were but she was acutely aware of the fact that Chandra could be executed for killing an Englishman; the legal system from the Protector to the magistrates leaned in favour of protecting the employers. If she did not engage the *Sahib* now then she would never forgive herself for not having tried her utmost to save an innocent man.

She cut a strange, lonely and incongruous figure as she walked barefooted towards the cottage amidst English men and women, who gathered in little groups, speaking in conspiratorial whispers.

At the door, she was stopped by a bearded Englishman who demanded the reason for her presence there. Although she did not understand, she surmised that he was questioning her presence at the cottage.

"*Sahib* — talk!" she said. Ann, who was at the cottage, noticed the odd figure of Baigum and stepped out to assist. Ann's association with Mary, the coolie maid, had equipped her sufficiently to understand Baigum's request. Claude, not without reluctance, allowed Baigum an audience. She was shown into a large room with a stone floor and a thatched roof. A large wooden table with wooden chairs were the only items of furniture. A candle, at the centre of the table cast a dim light, in the otherwise darkened room. Claude was seated with his elbow on the table, propping his chin. Baigum felt a little more at ease with Ann next to her.

"I don't know why I am talking to you at a time like this." He said. But Baigum understood nothing.

"Why do you want to see me?" he asked, trying to appear indifferent. Ann prodded Baigum gently to speak. Baigum began to speak in Hindi, punctuated with a few words in English. She spoke softly and calmly. But Claude understood very little. He stopped her after a short while and requested that Solomon, a *sirdar* who knew enough English to interpret, be present.

Claude knew that if Chandra was tried for the murder of his father, then he would reveal all the information that he had kept hidden all the while. It would be in his interest to do so. Any man who was facing the noose would reveal any information that had previously been concealed, hoping that it would serve in mitigation of sentence or better still, it would lead to his acquittal. The likelihood of the sordid details of his father's involvement in his mother's murder becoming public knowledge and the likelihood of it not being just village gossip but an established fact, after it is aired at a court hearing, steered him in the direction of caution. Solomon was able to interpret the series of events that led to the death of John Bennet as reported by Baigum, fairly accurately. Claude rubbed his eyes with his forefinger and thumb in contemplation. There was silence in the room. Baigum was praying earnestly. Ann walked across to Claude and put her arm comfortingly on his shoulder. She could sense that his mind was in turmoil.

"I need to speak to your husband. Where is he?" he said eventually.

Solomon interpreted and Baigum responded. But Claude knew that the village constabulary had only a holding cell. If he was going to speak to the Indian, he must act before Chandra was transferred. Soon he would be transferred either to Durban or Pietermaritzburg, where he would be held until the trial; then it would be extremely difficult to engage with the Indian, given the complexities of the bureaucracy of the day. Baigum was content, at least for the moment that the *Sahib* was going to engage with Chandra. She hoped that the *Sahib* would be convinced of Chandra's innocence and that he would use his influence to have her husband released.

Claude Bennet saddled his horse despite Ann's protests. His father's funeral was being held the following day. He knew that he had to speak to the Indian for his own sake; he needed to hear the truth from him. The uncertainty and the speculations around his father's role in his mother's death was a source of great anxiety and unease. He set off at a gallop to escape Ann's protests. The six mile distance to the village constabulary was less than an hour on horseback, without exhausting the horse.

He tethered the horse to an overhanging branch of a tree. The gravel crunched under his booted feet as he walked up the short path leading to the little building of the constabulary. Sergeant Greene and Constable Barney were poring over a sheaf of papers when they noticed Claude Bennet. They recognised him and Sergeant Greene stepped out from behind the counter with an extended arm.

"Don't worry Mr Bennet the coolie will pay for his atrocious deed." said the Sergeant while Constable Barney, not to be left out, added, "Oh Yes! We'll make sure of that!"

"I'm sure you would!" replied Claude, "But I'm here for something else."

"How can we help, Mr Bennet?" responded the Sergeant.

"I want to speak to the coolie, in private." replied Claude.

"Sir!" responded the Sergeant, "Given the fact that you are in an emotional state and very angry, I might add, it is not wise for us to accede to such a request."

"We can, however", continued the Sergeant, "allow you to speak to the coolie but in our presence."

Claude had not expected such resistance. He unholstered his Smith and Wesson revolver and placed it on the desk and invited them to frisk him.

"The bars will be separating us! I must speak to him in private, please!" Claude raised his hands, in submission, to be searched.

The Sergeant, after a moment's hesitation, turned towards his Constable and ordered him to accompany Claude to the cell.

"You have fifteen minutes, Sir!" the Sergeant called out after them as the Constable led Claude out towards the cell.

A large rat squeaked and scuttled across the cold stone floor and stopped to stare at Chandra with its beady eyes. Chandra sat crouched at the furthest corner from the bucket intended to be used as a toilet. Mathuray's last words, *"God has forsaken me at a time I need him the most!"* echoed in his head. At times he could almost see Mathuray clutching the bars in desperation and begging him to help him. It was at these times that he felt utterly helpless and contemplated death. Then his thoughts would wander to Baigum and his little girl and he would be filled with resolve and determination. He thought of his father, his mother and Kandan and smiled; he thought of the vast expanse of green fields, when times were good; he thought of the young maidens with coquettish smiles carrying clay-pots of water from the river and he would break into a chuckle. Then his mind would flash back to Shubnum and the love that they had shared, and he would recall in vivid detail the events leading up to her being jettisoned into the cold Indian Ocean and his body would shudder almost involuntarily.

He slept very little in the three days he had been there. With a coarse brown sack for a blanket and another that he folded to be used as a pillow, he lay on the cold stone floor, trying to shut off the nightmare. At times he almost believed that he was dreaming and then the stark reality would dawn on him; then he would sit on the floor, draw his knees up to his face and whimper piteously. It was at such a time that Claude saw Chandra in the cell.

Constable Barney took delight in rattling the bars of the cell with his baton. The loud sound did not evoke any sudden response from Chandra who appeared to have been numbed into insensitivity by inactivity and confinement. The Constable had to rattle the bars again before Chandra responded. Claude was taken aback by the man he saw. Chandra looked emaciated and appeared to have aged overnight. His face was covered with a fine stubble of grey, black and white beard. His cheeks had lost their fullness and his cheekbones assumed a new prominence, making him look cadaverous. His hair, like his beard was unkempt and dishevelled. His slightly discoloured white shirt appeared dirty and stained and hung loosely over his equally stained khaki trousers. He wore no shoes.

When Chandra recognised Claude he stumbled up to him, as fast as his weak state would allow him. Constable Barney walked back and they were alone.

"*Sahib!*" cried out Chandra, holding the bars, "Help me!"

"That depends!" responded Claude.

"*Sahib!* I not push the Master!"

"For me to help you, I need to know everything. Tell me what you saw on the morning of my mother's murder. My father is dead now. You need not be afraid."

Claude listened in rapt silence as the details unfolded. Somehow, the confirmation of his father's role in his mother's murder, lessened his grief. He felt lighter; he felt that destiny had played a role with its brand of justice. But the villainy and treachery of his father pricked his conscience with a thousand needles. That an innocent man should die through the deviousness and manipulations of his father, troubled him no small measure. That the blood of such a man was coursing through his veins made him feel repugnant. Yet, he felt the intense, instinctive and primeval need to protect the image of his family. Now, it was not important to him whether Chandra was guilty or not. But he had an intuitive feeling that the man was, indeed, innocent.

"I shall help you. But I want you to know that I am not the *only* player in determining your destiny. But I shall use my influence to help. You *do* know that the penalty for killing an Englishman, let alone an employer, is the death sentence." While Claude spoke Chandra listened quietly, nodding his head but there was no doubt that the man was in agony.

"However, I want you to help me!" continued Claude. "Do not tell anyone, least of all the court, what you have told me here today. As of now, this is village talk and gossip. This will be the last time you would have relayed the story!" Chandra nodded vigorously in agreement.

"Promise me!" demanded Claude.

"Sahib! I promise on the names of the people I love! Please help me!" Claude walked back to the Office of the constabulary, retrieved his revolver, shook hands with the sergeant and the constable and left.

Chandra's hands and feet were shackled when he was transferred to a prison in Durban in a caged horse-drawn cart. He found himself in a large courtyard with several others, most of whom were natives. He was directed to a cell, one of many adjoined to each other in a row. Although he welcomed the presence of people around him, none of them appeared to be friendly. It was the following day that he was escorted to appear before a magistrate. The magistrate was expected to assess the case before him to establish whether the case was serious enough to warrant a trial in which case the accused was committed to prison until the trial. There was no question of doubt that in Chandra's case there was sufficient evidence to merit a trial. Chandra was ignorant of the proceedings and expected to be given an opportunity to relate his story. When he was shown back to the cell he became extremely despondent.

He lost track of the days of the week. The routine was regimental and repeated daily. No single day was distinctive from another. But he was able to keep count of the number of days by plucking a strand of hair every morning and tying it around a wooden spoon which he kept tucked away under his pillow.

He had no news of Baigum and his little daughter and wondered whether he would ever get to see them again. In his mind's eye he saw his mother, his father, his brother Kandan and Shubnum. The thought of Shubnum tugged at his heart strings. His eyes grew misty — he could almost hear his father say, *"Do not go too close to the lion, my son. You will not survive the bite. Make your fortune and do not forget your family and return to us! The English will not be here forever! The good Lord will take care of things."* That was four years ago. He longed to be with Baigum and Parvathy again and resolved to work and save enough money to pay for their passage back to India. But he had to convince the justice system here that he was innocent. He wanted to pray but the words of Mathuray, "Where is this God?" echoed hauntingly and persistently,

---

Three weeks had gone by and Chandra had given up all hope. He had not heard from Baigum or Claude Bennet. The warden had informed him, however, that he was scheduled to appear before a judge and jury within a week. Chandra did not have any idea what to expect. While he felt relieved and looked forward to it, it was not without a fair amount of anxiety. Who was going to represent him? This was an Englishman's court where a coolie Indian was going to be tried for the murder of an Englishman— where the judge and jury were English. He felt as vulnerable as a rabbit pursued by a dozen greyhounds.

The day finally arrived. Chandra was led, with shackles, into a large room with rows of benches which were already occupied by men and women. The front end had a raised podium with a wooden table and a chair intended for the judge. Flanking the courtroom on the left were three rows of seating arranged in a stepped tier for the jury. On the left of the judge's table stood a little cubicle, much like a pulpit, intended for the witnesses.

When the judge, who sported a bushy black and grey moustache and who was attired in a black robe walked in, everyone in the courtroom stood up and resumed their seats only after the judge had taken his seat. Chandra was seated in the front row closest to the judge. He did not notice the familiar figure of Claude Bennet, smartly attired in a grey, pin striped suite, sitting on the same bench as he was, until Claude edged towards him. What Chandra did not know was that Claude Bennet was representing him.

The judged struck his gavel on the table three times to commence proceedings.

"Chandra Chosaran, you are being hereby charged for the murder of one, John Bennet, who was your employer, at the place of his residence on the 18 July 1864. How do you plead?"

A turbaned Indian standing between the witness stand and the jury translated into Hindi.

Chandra responded impulsively in loud incoherent tones with vigorous gesticulations. Claude signalled him to remain quiet by placing his index finger on his lips. Claude stood up and declared, "Your Honour! My client pleads not guilty!"

"State your name and status for the purposes of this Court, please," commanded the judge.

"Your Honour, I am Claude John Bennet and will be defending my client."

The judge interlaced his fingers and looked perplexed.

"Claude John Bennet? Amazing! Are you not the son of the victim?"

"That I am, your Honour." replied Claude.

"Then please regale me, Mr Bennet! I am pretty confused to say the least! Why are you choosing to defend the alleged perpetrator of such a heinous act against your very father?"

"Sir . . . . Your Honour! I have heard the defendant's story of the events leading to my father's death and I have reason to believe that he is innocent. If, indeed, there was foul play, then I *too* would like to see the perpetrator hanging at the end of a noose. But, Your Honour, I am a God fearing man, like yourselves, and I would not like to see an innocent man, however passionate we are to have the culprit apprehended, paying with his life for something he is not guilty of."

"Very interesting, Mr Bennet! And very eloquent indeed, I might add! But you do realise that you have a monumental task of convincing the Jury that your client is innocent."

The judge was now tapping the ends of his fingers of both his hands against each other in contemplation.

"Let us hear the prosecution!" declared the Judge. The prosecutor was a short bespectacled man with a fringe of hair around his bald pate.

"Thank you, Your Honour! I am intrigued by my colleague's optimism and display of confidence. The case against the accused is not a complicated one. The accused, Chandra Chosaran, Indenture Number. 24740, whom you see in the dock, was employed by John Bennet as a *sirdar* since 1862. The late John Bennet had been magnanimous. Not only did he afford the accused a cottage, he also allowed him the rare privilege of owning a horse. It is believed that the accused had grown greedy and had attempted to exploit the good nature of John Bennet; the accused was demanding an increase in his weekly stipend. I have a single witnesses who will bear testimony to the fact that the accused had become aggressive when John Bennet refused to accede to the Indian's demands. He had wilfully and with malicious intent shoved the victim, who was slightly inebriated at that time. John Bennet, may his Soul rest in peace, met with an untimely death at the hands of the accused. I shall call upon my only witness, the house maid, Tembi Makathini."

All this time the turbaned Indian interpreter was finding it extremely difficult to do justice to the interpretation for the prosecutor did not pause to accommodate the interpreter. Chandra struggled to comprehend.

Tembi waddled up to the witness box in her characteristic fashion.

A Zulu man with a pot belly, in a shabby suit stood next to the witness box to interpret.

"On the morning of July 18th of this year (for the purpose of court records it is 1864), you saw the accused with the late John Bennet?" The Zulu interpreted and Tembi responded after a bit of hesitation.

"Tell the court," the prosecutor continued, "the details of the meeting between your master and that man!" pointing towards Chandra, and Tembi spoke, haltingly in Zulu.

The master and Chaaandra were talking loudly. The master was angry. When the master is angry we don't go anywhere near. Then I went inside my house and closed the door. A little later, when the shouting and talking stopped, I came outside and I saw Chaaandra running away. I saw master—he had fallen. There was blood around his head." The Zulu interpreter translated but it was clear that the interpreter knew only a smattering of English. The turbaned Indian translated into Hindi.

"The accused ran because he had deliberately shoved the master down the stairs?" continued the prosecutor.

Claude interrupted with, "Objection, Your Honour! He is leading the witness!"

"Sustained!" responded the judge.

"Was there anyone else with the master when this took place?" asked the prosecutor.

Tembi shook her head and the Judge ordered her to answer the question.

"No! There was nobody else!" and the interpreters followed through.

"Thank you! No more questions!" said the prosecutor as he buttoned his coat and took his seat.

When Tembi stood up to leave, the judge ordered her to stay.

"Your witness, Mr Bennet!" said the judge. There was a hushed silence when Claude stood up. Claude was young and good looking. While the younger ladies took an interest in him for personal reasons, the others looked on with rapt attention, wondering what his line of defence would be. Despite Claude's earlier justification, they could not understand why anyone would want to defend a man alleged to be the killer of one's father.

"Tembi! How long have you worked for us?" asked Claude. But what impressed the court, was his competence in Zulu. He switched spontaneously to Zulu and repeated the question. The Zulu interpreter felt redundant. He responded with, "Haw!" a generic form of exclamation for everything from extreme shock to a pleasant surprise.

"*Five years!*" replied Tembi in Zulu. Claude looked at the Zulu interpreter to resume his function. The Zulu smiled in appreciation. All this while the turbaned Indian continued to intone in Hindi, unobtrusively.

"There is one thing I always respected — that's honesty." Claude resisted the temptation to repeat it in Zulu. Instead he glanced at the Zulu, who appeared to be more cautious about the interpretation.

"*Yes, Baas!*" replied Tembi, looking down and wringing her fingers, nervously.

"*Do not be afraid!*" Claude stated in Zulu.

"Your honour!" the prosecutor stood up from his seat, "I am sure we are all impressed with Mr Bennet's command of the native language. But I would urge Mr Bennet to desist from using Zulu in court."

"Mr Bennet!" the judge looked at Claude and waved his finger in mild admonition.

"Tembi!" continued Claude, "You saw Chandra on that day! Did you see him *run* or *walk*?" Tembi looked confused because she did not understand the line of questioning nor did she at any time make a concerted effort to make a distinction between the two actions. All the while she had been using the terms loosely to communicate the fact that she saw him leaving.

"*He was walking fast!*" she said in Zulu.

"What is the significance of your line of questioning Mr Bennet?" interrupted the judge.

"Your Honour, I am of the view that any man who had wilfully and deliberately killed another, is most likely to run away from the scene of the crime, as quickly as possible to avoid being incriminated. This, the defendant, had not done. He was seen walking away from a confrontation."

"Very well!" said the judge, "continue!"

"Was the *baas* drunk at the time?" Claude probed.

"The baas was drinking!" she replied.

"Yes! Tembi! He may have been drinking but *was* he *drunk?*" persisted Claude.

"Yes, he was drunk!" responded Tembi.

"How do you know?"

"He stood up to hit Chaaandra!" she continued in Zulu. By now Tembi had grown quite confident. She stood up and demonstrated the drunken stagger of John Bennet much to the amusement of the court. The judge too, seemed to have enjoyed the comic relief, but checked himself and rapped his gavel on his table and called for order.

"Enough of the histrionics!" he bellowed.

Tembi resumed her seat and Claude continued.

"Tell us what happened, thereafter!"

"I saw Chaaandra leave and I went inside. I heard a sound and came out and I saw Chaaandra far away and the baas had fallen!"

Claude was pleased with Tembi's testimony. In fact, he had received more information crucial to the case than he had expected. When the Zulu interpreter translated, Claude saw the need to correct or add to the translation because he had failed to capture salient information adequately.

"Tembi! Did you see Chandra touch or push the *baas?*" Claude asked.

"No!" replied Tembi.

"Gentlemen of the Jury," Claude faced the grim faced men of the Jury, "the *prima facie* evidence that resulted in the defendant being arraigned for murder, in the first instance was purely circumstantial. Nobody had seen the defendant push the victim — that was purely speculative. But the new evidence, as has been testified by the witness, indicates that the defendant was already several yards away when the victim had the fatal fall. Given the fact that John Bennet had consumed a fair amount of liquor, it is a plausible explanation that he had lost balance and had fallen. I submit that no one was responsible for my father's . . . . I beg your pardon, for John Bennet's death. He had brought it upon himself! Gentlemen of the Jury, every one of you is a God fearing man. The defendant is clearly innocent! In our quest to seek justice let us not err by allowing an innocent man to hang at the end of a noose."

"Impressive, Mr Bennet!" remarked the judge. "Let us hear the case for the prosecution."

The prosecutor, strode over to the Jury while Claude resumed his seat.

"Gentlemen of the Jury! Firstly, I am intrigued by the fact that the son of the victim should defend the accused! Despite his very eloquent justification, I am inclined to believe that there is more to this than meets the eye. Gentlemen of the Jury, are we going to acquit the coolie Indian based on the testimony of a native? It is common knowledge that both groups of people, the coolies and the natives, are prone to lying and deceit. The witness, is a heathen and has no moral or religious compulsion to adhere to the dictates of the Bible or the injunctions of the Law and as such I submit that the testimony of the witness be declared null and void."

The judge raised his eyebrows in bewilderment.

"Do you realise that if the court does not acknowledge the credibility of the witness and negates her testimony that *exonerates* the accused then we shall be obliged to negate the testimony that *incriminates* him. The accused is in court purely on the testimony of Tembi Makathini. I do not want to pre-empt nor influence the decision of the Jury, but you have, and I do believe unwittingly, created a contradiction in your argument. However, the guilt or innocence of the defendant, should be independent of the degree of competence of persons prosecuting or defending. It is therefore incumbent upon the jury to deliberate without prejudice or emotion in order to reach a fair and objective decision!"

The court adjourned for the day and the members of the jury were ushered into a room where they were locked in deliberation for more than an hour.

There were arguments and counter-arguments. While the rhetoric declared that deliberations must be free of prejudice and it must be fair, the reality was that it was a colonial English court made up of Englishmen trying an indentured coolie for the murder of an Englishman. Behind the closed doors, much was said in private that would not be uttered in public. Some even ventured to say that finding the accused innocent would send a dangerous message to other would be offenders.

"We have to set an example!" declared one member of the Jury.

"But the coolie is clearly innocent!" retorted another.

"Yes! He may not have been directly responsible for the death of John Bennet, but he would not have died, had the coolie not *incensed* him to the point where he had lost his self-composure!" argued one.

"For God's sake! He was *drunk!*" countered a member of the jury who appeared to be the village parson.

Finally, they all agreed, some reluctantly, that Chandra Chosaran was guilty of murder but a mitigatory factor being that the act was not premeditated.

Chandra returned to his cell. For the first time in many weeks he felt light-hearted and hopeful. He recalled the events of the day and his respect and admiration for Claude Bennet reached new heights. The combination of his understanding of the English language and the Hindi from the interpreter had allowed him to have had a fairly good insight into the court hearings. He was optimistic that if justice prevailed then he would be a free man soon. He sat on the crude bed of his little cell and planned and projected how he would conduct his life hereafter—and a glimmer of a smile appeared on his face. He imagined himself with Baigum and Parvathy. He would save enough money to pay for the passage back to India. He would till the fields and work hard but he would not be a slave to any man. Such were his thoughts when the warden appeared, opened the door and gestured to him to follow. Chandra found himself in the courtroom again. This time, there were very few people in the court; the Jury was not present. The rows of benches were mostly empty. Claude Bennet was present together with the prosecutor. The turbaned Indian interpreter was also present. When the Judge walked in, everybody stood up, more as a perfunctory gesture than a show of respect and the Judge waved his hand for them to be seated.

Chandra was shackled at the wrist and ankles. The Judge ordered him to stand and step forward. All he heard were, "Guilty!" and "Twenty-five years!" Everything else the Judge said were a string of meaningless sounds to him. He looked around blankly and appeared to be unaware of his surroundings. While a court official held him at the shoulder and led him away, Claude Bennet sat on the bench, his elbows on his lap and clutching his head in despair. He realised that he had been a fool to expect the justice system of this Colony to be devoid of prejudices; he realised that the colonial Englishman would always seek to maintain a rigid hierarchical structure to ensure his own survival. He had invited Baigum to both the court hearings and the pronouncement of the verdict. She had refused, stating that the experience would be too traumatic for her. Claude felt somewhat relieved that she had not been present.

When he reached his cottage later that day he sent Tembi to summon Baigum. While he waited, he kept pacing up and down, pondering how he was going to break the news of her husband's sentence to her. He had also requested Ann to be present. Then his thoughts flitted to Ann; recently he had neglected her. He heard the door creak as it opened slowly and Ann entered. He hugged her and pecked her on the cheek and then related the events from the court hearing to the pronouncement of the verdict. There was a knock on the door and Tembi ushered in Baigum. The bands around her ankles tinkled as she padded her way barefooted into the room. Baigum smiled at Ann as she took her seat at the table. Ann had a rudimentary understanding of Hindi, which she had gathered from Mary, the coolie maid.

"Where is my husband?" Baigum enquired in Hindi. With a combination of English, Hindi and gesticulations, they were able to communicate Chandra's fate. Baigum lapsed into silence. Then she held the end of her *sarie* to her face and wept.

Claude Bennet had arranged for Baigum and her daughter to visit Chandra at the prison in Durban. He had made available a horse-drawn cart and a native servant to escort them. They left very early, before the sun could appear over the eastern horizon. The journey was uneventful but they were painfully tired after four hours.

Chandra's hands and feet were shackled. A warden escorted him as he dragged his feet slowly along the stone floor of the passage. He entered a large empty room with just a table and two chairs. Baigum was seated on the chair with Parvathy on her lap. She would not have recognised her husband if she had not expected him through the door. His hair was long and matted. His grey beard was a forest of limp strands. The bones of his face appeared elevated and prominent against his sunken cheeks. His daughter made no attempt to run to him like she usually did. Instead, she gaped uncomprehendingly at the man before her. Chandra would have preferred not to be seen by his family in his present condition—but it was too late.

"How are you and my little girl?" he asked in Hindi as he reached out to caress his daughter's cheek, but she pulled away.

Baigum admonished her gently, saying, *"It is papa, beti! Go to papa!"* and she released Parvathy to go to her father. The child walked towards her father but not with the same enthusiasm as before. He held her little head towards his chest and his eyes grew misty.

"My father said to me, 'Don't go too close to the lion!' I never listened!" Baigum sobbed silently as he spoke.

"I know that everything you did, you did for us! She reached out and clasped his shackled hand, and the feel of the cold metal somehow befitted the desperate situation in which they found themselves.

"Remember we said that Parvathy should have a baby brother or sister as a companion?" she smiled, amidst her sobs.

"Yes! We were so happy! But that will never happen now." he remarked.

"Yes! It's going to happen! she said, crying and smiling at the same time. *"I am expecting your baby! That was one of the reasons I did not want to be at the court hearings!"* His eyes brightened. He would have loved to hug her and tell her how much he loved her but the weight of the shackles was a grim reminder that their destiny was chartered differently. He closed his eyes and prayed silently, *"Dear Lord! My child will grow up without a father! I know that I will not endure twenty-five years in this God forsaken place! Give them the strength, the will and the resolve to survive!"*

She squeezed his hand to bring him back. *"God will bring you back to us, my husband and we will be happy again!"* He looked at her piercingly.

"God? What God? Where is this God that deems it fit to treat his children thus? And then he realised that he uttered the words almost as if they were from a script and remembered Mathuray's last words.

"Go back to India!" he whispered.

"I will not leave without you!" she countered.

"Twenty-five years is a long time to wait. You are young and now you have added responsibilities. You do not have much of a choice! You must go back!"

"I miss you so much!" she cried, *"the cottage feels cold and empty without you!"* and she used the end of her sarie to dab the tears from her eyes. Parvathy stretched her small hands to wipe her mother's tears and Chandra's heart melted.

"We should not forsake God!" she whispered.

He almost responded but resisted as the memories of his last meeting with Mathuray flooded his mind in graphic detail and the words echoed in his head, *"I left Bharat but I never left God."*

The prison warden entered, announcing that it was time for the visitors to leave. Chandra stood up to hug them both but he realised that he was hindered by the shackles.

"Take care of my children and speak well of me! Tell them I loved them." he shouted as he was led away. Even Baigum's optimism and confidence seemed to waver. She continued staring after him wondering if she would ever see him again and felt an overwhelming emptiness within her.

EPILOGUE

Baigum left the prison, after seeing Chandra, with a heart laden with sorrow. Somehow, she knew that she would never get to see him again. Claude Bennet, on hearing of her pregnant state, had employed her with light duties as Tembi's assistant. She had just over a year for her five-year contract to expire. In September of that year she delivered a bonny baby boy. Despite the baby's infancy she was able to discern that he looked like his father. She named him Chand in memory of his father. Her life at the Bennet household was comfortable.

Ann, whom Claude had married, was good and kind to her. In fact, Ann had found a friend and companion in her. Although Baigum had not accumulated enough money to pay her way and that of her children, for the return passage to India, Ann had no difficulty in convincing her husband to subsidise the cost. Baigum returned to India and lived as a single parent for the rest of her life.

Chandra resigned himself to his fate. He lived with memories. Within a year of his imprisonment he had fallen ill. He did not recover and died shortly after. He was buried in an unmarked grave without any ceremony.

Harold Croft had his leg amputated. His equestrian activities ceased completely and he had never forgiven the Indians.

Mary Gabriel married Peter Solomon and had many children. They were able to join the ranks of free Indians and made significant progress in business.

Parvathy married an Indian soldier in the British army. Her children loved the stories she related of their grandfather, Chandra, in a far off place called Natal. Parvathy's brother, Chand grew up to be the image of his father. He doted on his mother, Baigum. Often, she would notice his general demeanour and mannerisms and wonder at how much alike he was to his father. Her mind would hark back to her husband and tears would stream down her face. But her thoughts were private and beautiful. Her grandchildren would clamour around her and ask, *"Why are you crying, ma?"* and she would say, *"I am thinking of a good man who played too close to the lion! Too close to the lion!"*

MEANINGS OF
NON-ENGLISH WORDS

Beti: A term of fondness for a younger person, literally interpreted as a "little girl"

Feringhees: A term used to refer to the colonial whites in India
Lota: A bowl used by the Indians for ablutions

Kanganis: Recruiters of labour

Bhaiya: Hindi word for brother

Zamindari and ryotwari: This system demanded that a percentage of the gross produce of the agricultural land be paid as tax to the British colonial Government

Bharat - India
Sirdar - an Indian supervisor on the sugarcane field
Kurta - loose fitting cultural outfit worn by Indian males